D0891518

MAKING OVER MAGGIE

A

Women of Surprise

Romance

Other books by Tracey J. Lyons:

Lydia's Passion
A Surprise for Abigail

MAKING OVER MAGGIE

•

Tracey J. Lyons

AVALON BOOKS
NEW YORK

Library of Congress Catalog Card Number: 2004099736
ISBN 0-8034-9726-1

Published by Thomas Bouregy & Co., Inc.
160 Madison Avenue, New York, NY 10016

PRINTED IN THE UNITED STATES OF AMERICA
ON ACID-FREE PAPER
BY HADDON CRAFTSMEN, BLOOMSBURG, PENNSYLVANIA

This one is dedicated to the memory of my grandmother, Lina Davis.
If not for the many loving summers spent in Waterloo, NY, the Women of Surprise would never have come to be.

Special thanks to my editor for this series, Erin Nuimata. I'm glad we share the same vision for Abigail, Lydia, and Maggie!

Chapter One

Catskill Mountains
New York State
1883

Thunder rumbled off in the distance. Samuel Clay looked over his shoulder. Heavy, dark storm clouds loomed behind him, breaking through the craggy peaks and narrow valleys of the Catskill Mountains.

Taking the crumpled piece of paper from his coat pocket, he tried to make sense of the directions. If the map was right, he was almost to the town of Surprise, New York. Fat drops of water splattered intermittently onto the hard packed earth. Samuel's horse shook his head from side to side. Even the beast sensed the impending storm.

He stuffed the map back into his pocket. Hunching over the saddle, Samuel pushed the animal onward, hoping to reach shelter before the clouds broke and the rain let loose. Following the path of the train tracks, he continued to search for any sign of life and was about to give up hope when two outbuildings appeared before him.

Like an apparition, he thought. One minute he was feeling lost and alone in this forsaken rocky wilderness and the next he was entering the main road of a small town. *Surprise!* he thought ruefully. Whoever had named the town must have had quite a wry sense of humor.

Sam wasn't looking for any surprises. This town was his last chance to prove himself. He'd seen the advertisement for a dance hall manager in the Albany newspaper. After making the proper contacts, he'd been offered the job on the condition that the owner of the hall approved of him.

Right now, though, he was sorely in need of a dry place to stay and a good hot meal. Because of the coming storm there wasn't much activity on the streets. He saw two women hurry into a building with a sign proclaiming it to be Jules' Mercantile.

Scanning the narrow street, Sam took notice of a lumberyard, a small café, one sheriff's office, a boarding house, and finally a large two-story square building.

While the latter held his attention, he thought the first order of business should be securing a room at the boarding house. Nudging the horse with his knee, Samuel Clay sat tall in his saddle as he rode through the town of Surprise taking in every nuance.

Looking off to the left he saw a schoolhouse, but what caught and held his attention was the grand house that seemed to fill the space at the end of the road.

Whistling softly, Samuel slowed the horse and took a closer gander at the elegant three-story house. Stonework blended with wood siding. A well-tended yard surrounded the structure with forsythias and rose bushes dotting the foundation.

"Hold up right there, mister."

Startling him out of his musings the feminine command brought him to a stop in the middle of the roadway. Looking down the horse's long neck and past the perked ears, Samuel found himself gazing at the nicely rounded backside of a woman.

Dressed all in black he thought she just might

be the town spinster. He pulled the thin leather reins to the right and the horse began to move past the woman.

A stiff raised hand shot up. "I said, hold up."

She didn't even turn to look at him and this compelled him to follow her gaze. Her attention was clearly on what had to be one of the ugliest signs he'd ever laid eyes upon. Black paint that had been applied with a heavy hand spelled out the words *Dance Hall* on a dark green background.

"A little to the left, Cole," the sharp voice commanded.

"More to the left," Samuel offered with a grin. When it looked as if the hideous sign was about to fall off the building he added, "Yeah, that looks real good to me."

This caught her attention. Hands on hips she spun around to face him, fury burning in her light blue eyes. Surprise forced him to cough out the breath he'd been holding.

She was a young woman! From her starchy appearance, he'd been certain that she was an older woman, one nearing her thirtieth year. Instead he found himself staring at a woman who couldn't be more than twenty if she were a day.

"I beg your pardon, sir, but I don't recall asking for your opinion."

Huffy young thing she was. Quickly Sam

amended his impression of her. From her starchy attitude she could be going on thirty. "Just thought I'd offer an impartial opinion. That is one ugly sign, ma'am."

The man holding the sign laughed as if to say, "I told you so." Ignoring him, she pinned her stare on Samuel.

"I'll have you know that I came up with the design."

"She's not very creative, is she?" Sam looked up at the gentleman and grinned.

"Don't insult me."

Sam didn't see his comment as an insult; he was just being honest. The thick block lettering was a simply thought out design. It would never draw attention to the dance hall, the new enterprise in this town.

"If you expect people to come to this building they need something with some flare. Colors that will capture their attention and make them want to wander over and see what's inside."

"And you know this how?" Advancing on him, she stood close to the horse right by Samuel's left leg. He didn't think that now would be a good time to tell her that he was going to be the manager of this here establishment.

Shrugging, he answered, "I've traveled around a lot. I've seen establishments like this before."

"This is not just any other establishment, mister. This is a dance hall." Pointing at the sign as if he were a complete idiot, she added, "See, those words spell out *Dance Hall*. And it's going to be the best one for miles around."

"Yes, you are right, it does say *Dance Hall*." Of course he'd been teasing her. He never could resist getting a rise from any young lady.

Rain dripping from the brim of his hat, Samuel leaned over and said to the woman, "If you don't mind, Miss . . ." the word, an invitation to an introduction, hung in the air.

"Monroe. My name is Miss Maggie Monroe."

"Well, Miss Monroe, I'm getting wet and I'd really like to be moving to someplace where I can get dry. So if it's all right with you, I'd like to pass." He couldn't resist adding a wink to his request.

Staring up at him with blue eyes, she looked as if he'd asked for a brick of gold, not to get inside out of the rain.

With a quick swish of her hand she dismissed him. "Yes. You can move along, Mister . . . ?" With one fine brown eyebrow raised she waited for him to tell her his name.

"Samuel Clay." He was more than happy to oblige her since—at least in his mind—they were going to be business partners.

Picking up her voluminous black skirts, she stepped up onto the planked walkway under the shelter of a gray striped awning.

Sitting tall in the saddle, Samuel tipped his hat to her. "See you around, Miss Monroe."

"Good day, Mr. Clay."

Within an hour's time, Samuel had boarded the horse at the local stable and secured himself a room at Bartholomew's boarding house. Standing at the frilly lace curtained window of his room, he watched the activity at the dance hall through the mist of rain.

The first thing he noticed was that the sign had come down. So Miss Monroe did care about public perception. It just so happened that Sam cared about the same thing. One's appearance was the first thing anyone noticed about a person. A business or businessman wasn't any different.

First impressions were what success or failure hinged upon. He'd learned that valuable life lesson at a very early age. His family may have led the simple life of farmers, but his mama always made sure they were dressed in clean clothing. And on the rare occasions when they went into town it was in their Sunday finest.

Gathering his overcoat, he paused in front of a full-length mirror. From the tips of his recently polished boots and pressed black trousers to the crisply starched white shirt showing beneath a richly colored black and gold brocade vest, Samuel Clay was a fine man who knew he presented a memorable first impression. If his mama could see him now, she'd be proud.

His first order of business upon deciding to come to Surprise had been to ship two trunks of belongings on ahead. Finding Mrs. Bartholomew sitting at a writing desk in the front parlor, he inquired as to the location of the post office.

"I hope you found everything to your satisfaction, Mr. Clay."

"I did, thank you, ma'am. I was wondering if you could point me in the direction of the post office."

Rising from the straight-backed chair, she walked with him to the front door. "It's at the opposite end of town. Right past the sheriff's office, Mr. Clay."

The screen door tapped shut behind him. Pausing for a moment on the front porch, Samuel's gaze was drawn to the mansion on the hill behind the boarding house. Droplets of rain glistened on the square-cut stonework. Tall windows flanked a large entryway.

His bags could wait. Turning toward the big house, he walked up the sloping slate walkway. Samuel swallowed hard, beating down a bad case of nerves. This job was his last chance. If plans went the way he hoped they would, maybe one day soon he too would be living the high life.

Going up the steps, he paused before the massive front door, picking up the brass lion-head knocker and letting it drop on the polished wood. Within minutes he was granted admittance.

The inside of the home was even more stunning than the outside. Family portraits hung on the wall going up the grand staircase to the second and third floors. Thick carpeting covered the wide-planked floor boards.

"Are you Mr. Clay?"

"I am," he nodded.

"Miss Margaret has been expecting you, sir," a tall, thin, dark-haired woman told him. "Follow me."

Walking down the first floor hallway, Sam had to bite his lower lip to keep from whistling out loud. This was by far the grandest home he'd ever been in and one that certainly stood out in this town like a diamond in the rough.

He wondered about the woman who lived here. Margaret Monroe Sinclair sat in a wing-backed chair in front of a stone hearth. Beside her was a low stand with a full tea service on it.

Samuel was served hot tea with lemon and blueberry scones all the while listening to the older woman instruct him on his new duties. After eliciting from him the fact that he'd never been jailed—obviously there was some history of this with previous employees—she welcomed him to the town and wished him well in his new job.

"Oh and one more thing, Mr. Clay, you'll be working with my niece, Maggie."

Choking on the gulp of tea he'd just about swallowed, Sam stared at the woman. She expected him to work side by side with that unimaginative young lady?

"Is that so," he drawled, thinking how some things were never as simple as they seemed.

With a nod of her head she answered him, and so it was that thirty minutes later he exited the house smiling. Inside those walls lived a woman who knew exactly what she wanted from life and how to go about getting it. It didn't matter where a man came from, it was where he was now that was important. And Samuel Clay was right where he wanted to be.

He had six months remaining on his time. Six months in which to prove himself a man. Thinking about that long ago day gave Sam a feeling of melancholy. There had never been any question that the oldest son in the Clay family would, when he reached the age of twenty-five, take over the farm.

For three generations that was how it was done, until Sam came along. Farming was a decent way to make a living, if a man were cut out for the job. But he'd known from an early age that farming wasn't in his blood, so he'd made a deal with his father two and a half years ago, man to man. If, after three years, Sam could make a go of it on his own, he wouldn't have to take over the family farm. If he failed, he would return home and run the farm with no complaints.

Stepping off the neatly kept porch, he walked along the main street, carefully avoiding any mud puddles. The rain had stopped and the sunshine had returned. Steamy clouds rose from the dampened earth, giving the town an ethereal appearance. Surprise was indeed his last hope . . . his last chance.

Passing by the dance hall, he heard the sound of voices raised in anger coming from within. He'd gone four paces beyond the building when curiosity got the best of him. Turning around, he walked back. Since the door was already partly open, he didn't wait for an invitation to enter.

"The colors for this sign are the ones that I want!"

"Maggie, they are too drab," the man he'd seen earlier helping Miss Monroe was saying.

"I don't care what you or that stranger thinks,

if I'd wanted your opinions I would have asked for them." Stamping her foot, she promptly folded her arms across her chest and raised her chin defiantly.

"No doubt about it," the man scoffed, "you are the most stubborn of the Monroe women."

Clearing his throat, Samuel started to approach them. "I hope I'm not interrupting."

Spinning around, she glared at him. "As a matter of fact you are. This is a private conversation."

"You could've fooled me. I think the entire town could hear you two carrying on with your lovers' spat."

"Lovers' what?" Miss Monroe shouted the question. "This isn't my husband! Cole is my cousin by marriage." Glowering at him, she added, "He's married to the sheriff. So you'd best be watching yourself around here, mister."

Like he cared one bit that she was threatening him. Grinning cockily, he stepped up to the bar where the sign under discussion lay. "I'll try to remember my manners."

From the other side of the bar, the man offered his hand. "Cole Stanton."

Shaking his hand, Sam said, "Pleased to meet you. My name's Samuel Clay."

"Sorry about my cousin, she seems to have forgotten *her* manners."

"I heard that!" Careful to avoid them, she stood at the far end of the bar. "Thank you for your help, Cole. I believe that I can take it from here."

With a quick shrug he walked from behind the bar. Leaning in close to Samuel, he warned, "I'd watch yourself around her if I were you."

Nodding his thanks, Sam turned to find Miss Monroe's attention riveted on him. He figured now would be as bad a time as any to spring the surprise on her.

Chapter Two

Maggie couldn't help staring at the man who was leaning against her bar. One elbow was lazily propped on the pitted slab of wood, while he had one foot resting on the tarnished copper pole that ran along the floor.

His dark pants were a sharp contrast to his richly colored vest. His short blond hair was parted in the middle and he wore muttonchops and a beard. She couldn't help but wonder how liberally he applied the ever-popular bay rum, used by more and more men these days, to promote hair growth.

Sniffing the air for the telltale scent, she was about to ask him to leave when he spoke.

"So this here's going to be a dance hall?" He looked around the room with a proprietary air, like he had ideas of his own for the building.

His pompous attitude was making her develop an intense dislike for the man. She wished he would leave. There was a great deal of work to be accomplished here today and she was already an hour behind.

Pointing to the sign resting not two inches away from his elbow, she said, "Good to know you can read, Mr. Clay. It should come in handy when you decide which direction to head when you leave Surprise."

Wandering away from the bar area, he walked slowly around the large room. "You have a very peculiar way of making a person feel welcome, ma'am."

There was no time for this nonsense. Maggie had so much to get done to prove to her aunt that this latest business venture would yield success. A great deal was resting on her shoulders and she was made acutely aware of this fact every day.

Just seeing how happy and successful her two cousins, Abigail, the town's sheriff and Lydia, the schoolteacher, were provided enough reminders of her own inadequacies. She certainly didn't need Mr. Clay here lollygagging about taking up her precious time.

"What are you going to do with this stage area?" He stood with his back to her, hands on his narrow hips looking at the broken-down stage.

Many of the wide wooden planks were warped from getting wet whenever the roof leaked. The stage had been used years ago to showcase local talent in the former monthly talent shows. Now that the old Grange Hall was under renovations her Aunt Margaret had taken to reminiscing about the shows.

Thanks to a generous donation by Alexander Judson, owner of the lumber mill, the roof had been repaired last month. The floorboards were going to be ripped out and replaced next week. At least she wouldn't have to worry about the recent rainfall ruining all of the work being done to the interior of the hall.

A fresh coat of white paint had been applied to all of the walls. The ceiling had been repainted too, and the cracked mirror behind the bar had been replaced with a more ornate one with a scrolled frame. The bar and the stage were the last of the major projects.

Maggie's hope was to have the dance hall open to the public in two weeks time. No decision had been made for the stage area as yet, and the bar would be transformed into a refreshment area. Lemonade and root beer would be served along with tea cookies.

She'd been busy lining up the first of their musicians. A trio from Albany would be arriving early next week. The upright piano from Aunt Margaret's front parlor would be moved here in a few days.

All in all, Maggie was pleased with the way things were progressing. Now she just had to rid herself of this pesky stranger and then she could finish today's chores.

Speaking to the man's back, she inquired lightly, "Mr. Clay, if there's nothing else, I really need to get back to work."

He swished his hand in the air as if to ward off a mosquito. "Oh, don't mind me, Miss Monroe."

"I'm afraid you don't understand. I work better by myself." Her patience wearing thin, Maggie walked toward him.

Just as she was about to tap him on the shoulder, he spun around to face her, startling her. Blue-green eyes stared back at her.

"This is a wonderful building, perfect for our new venture."

Several minutes passed before she found her voice. "Excuse me, but did I hear you say, *our* new venture? What would make you say such a thing, Mr. Clay?"

Grinning at her with raised eyebrows, he replied, "I was hired as the manager."

And with that the man turned, striding out of the building. Gathering her skirts she chased after him. "Wait! What did you just say?"

"I believe you heard me, Miss Monroe."

"Who hired you?"

Without so much as a backward glance, he said, "The lovely woman in the big house."

Quickly changing direction, Maggie hurried along to her aunt's. Anger roiled through her. She shook with it. Spots danced in front of her eyes from it.

She headed right up the hill and barged into Aunt Margaret's house like a thousand hounds were nipping at her heels.

Anna was dusting the sideboard in the hallway. Dust rag poised in mid-motion, she asked, "Miss Maggie, whatever is the matter?"

"Where is she?" Sure that by now her face was red and splotchy and frankly not caring a whit, she charged past the housekeeper. She knew where to find her aunt at this time of the day.

"Aunt Margaret! You had no right interfering in my business." Pausing in the doorway to the back parlor she took in the scene spread before her.

Aunt Margaret was lying on the sofa with a blanket spread across her lap. One arm was draped over her forehead while the other lay over her middle. The woman was as white as a ghost.

Long ago suspecting that her aunt's illness was feigned, Maggie forced herself to draw in a deep breath, just in the event this episode might be real, before proceeding into the room.

Slowly, forcing herself to take her time, she walked over to Aunt Margaret. Kneeling on the carpeted floor beside her, Maggie spoke through a jaw clenched in anger. "I know you hired Mr. Clay. I want to know one thing—why?"

Pale, almost transparent eyelids popped open. "You always were the straightforward one."

It really didn't matter to Maggie if her aunt were faking this illness. She would love her no matter what she did. Over the past year this woman had single-handedly brought life back into a dying town.

She even managed to bring Abigail, Lydia, and Maggie here to find true happiness and in the case of the former two, to find true love. Through all of this, though, Maggie didn't want her aunt to interfere in her life in the same manner.

Maggie always thought she was different than her cousins. She was single-minded in what she wanted from life. She wanted to be independent, knowing that if required to, she could live life on her own and provide for herself. After she'd accomplished that, then she would fall in love and get married.

Maggie didn't care that those thoughts weren't popular, but they were hers alone and no one—not her aunt, and certainly not someone like Mr. Clay—was going to change her mind.

Taking hold of her aunt's hand, she looked into those watery blue eyes.

"You can't interfere in my life the way you did Abby's and Lydia's."

"I'm doing no such thing."

"Then why did you hire him?"

"Maggie, several weeks ago as I recall, you told me that you would set up the dance hall and then once it was running you might be moving on."

Closing her eyes, she thought back to the day. It was close to two weeks ago and she'd been mad because she hadn't been consulted about the sign, among other things. In anger she may have intimated at leaving.

"You know full well I would never leave here and yet you went on ahead, without discussing it with me, and hired this man."

"Samuel Clay," the old woman said as if Maggie could forget his name.

"Yes, Samuel Clay."

Pushing up on one elbow, Aunt Margaret smiled. "I think he'll be perfect for the job."

"Fire him."

"I can't do that."

"Why not?"

"Because I need to be sure that you're going to stay committed to refurbishing the dance hall. A manager will keep you on task."

"I don't need anyone looking over my shoulder and double-checking every little thing that I do."

Sighing, Aunt Margaret replied, "I know you don't, but what you do need is someone who knows this business. And that someone is Mr. Clay."

Laying her head back against the sofa arm, she closed her eyes. "Make this work, Maggie. Do it for me."

And with those last four words she was dismissed. Choking back her frustration, she smoothed down the front of her skirts and left the house.

On the walk back to the hall, Maggie began to worry that all of her carefully laid plans would end up by the wayside. Knowing that men liked to take charge, she stiffened her shoulders preparing for battle.

Up for the challenge of dealing with a partner, for this was how she was going to think of Mr. Clay, Maggie set about deciding on the final color for the slab of thick wood which would serve as the refreshment area counter. She wanted the new wood to blend with the old and hoped that Alexander would be able to mix up a medium color stain. Then she would have to rush off to the mercantile to place an order for the linen tablecloths and napkins she'd picked out last week.

The teacups, dessert plates, and glasses were supposed to be arriving today. She still needed to find a place to store them where the workers wouldn't break the fragile items. Walking through the large room, Maggie pushed open a door that stood near the back.

Wiping a few cobwebs off of her face, she peered into the room. This would be a perfect storage area. She could have one of Mr. Jules' workers bring the boxes in here. Perfect. Backing out of the room, she turned her attention to the windows. They would need some sort of adornment and she knew just the person to consult with.

Grabbing her bonnet from the hook near the swinging doors, Maggie set off to visit her cousin Lydia. Careful to avoid the mud puddles, she picked her way across the street, taking the well-worn path that led to Lydia's new home.

Lydia had married the mill owner, Alexander Judson, last month. With two simple words, "I do," she'd become a wife and a mother. A widower, Alexander had been left with a son and a daughter to raise. Near as Maggie could tell her cousin was blissfully happy in her new life.

Even though most people suspected Maggie was envious of her cousins, she wasn't in the least. Maggie had her head and heart set on running a very successful business. Right now the most single-minded desire she had was to get the dance hall opened.

When she arrived at Lydia's the sounds of humming greeted her. Peering through the open window at the front of the home she caught a glimpse of Lydia. Her cousin was happily bustling about the kitchen. If the sweet homey smells wafting from within were any indication, Lydia was busy baking.

After a light knock on the front door, Maggie let herself in. Bowls and pans littered the small counter space in the kitchen. The smell of chocolate permeated the air.

Turning at the sound of her footsteps, the batter-laden spoon Lydia had been licking clattered in the sink. "Maggie! What a nice surprise! I didn't expect to see you standing there."

Lydia smiled, coming to greet Maggie with a hug. With a twinkle in her green eyes and wisps of fine red hair curled about her face and along the nape of her neck, Maggie thought Lydia looked radiant.

"I need some advice."

Chapter Three

"I hope this advice has to do with a man. It's time you settled down. You're too serious about this dance hall, Maggie. I'm worried about you."

Taking her by the hand, Lydia pulled Maggie along into the kitchen. "Sit," she directed, pointing to a chair at the head of the table.

Doing as she was told, Maggie pasted a smile on her face, trying to hide her annoyance. She was tired of her family inferring she needed a man to be happy. Just this morning, before she'd gone and hired that man, Aunt Margaret had made mention of the fact that Maggie would be in need of an entire wardrobe if she were to be the hostess for the hall. And bright colors were specifically suggested.

What she would choose to wear remained to be seen. There hadn't been a moment to spare this week, and her first concern was getting the hall finished by the self-imposed deadline.

Accepting the cup of tea Lydia was handing her, Maggie said, "Actually, I'm getting ready to put the finishing touches on the hall and I need your advice on curtains."

Sitting in the chair opposite her, Lydia smiled. "All right, where are these curtains going to be hung?"

"I was thinking of doing some type of sheer panels on all the windows. That way the patrons won't feel as if they are in a fishbowl. And, people strolling by the building would still be able to see inside. Hopefully they'll want to come inside and join in the fun."

Nodding, Lydia added some milk to her tea. "I like the idea. I saw some creamy white-colored sheer material at the mercantile last week. If Mr. Jules still has it, you should buy the entire bolt from him."

"I'll add the material to my list." Maggie was silent for a moment and then she said, "Aunt Margaret hired a manager for the dance hall."

Eyebrows raised, Lydia looked at Maggie. "Are you serious?"

"I am. She up and hires this man without so much as consulting with me. A perfect stranger! He rode into town this morning. I was working with Cole earlier; we were trying to hang the sign out in front of the hall and this man practically runs me down."

"And just how did he come to be hired by our aunt?"

"Apparently she took to heart a comment I made last week about getting this latest project done and then leaving."

Alarm showed clearly on Lydia's face. "You're leaving?"

"Of course I'm not leaving. I was having a bad day. She hired Mr. Clay because she wants to make sure the hall gets finished."

"Hmm. This is getting very interesting indeed."

"He came back to the hall a couple of hours later and was looking around like he owned the place. And then he ever so casually announces that he's going to be the new manager."

Rising from her chair, Lydia gathered their cups and saucers. "Hmm."

"I'm so close to being finished distractions are the last thing I need right now."

The cups and saucers clattered in the sink. "So this stranger is a distraction."

Maggie spun around in her seat. "I didn't say that. I don't know the man."

"Yes, but perhaps you might want to get to know him."

"Lydia there isn't any time in my life for such foolishness. The dance hall requires my full attention."

Maggie never ceased wondering about her cousins and how easily they were distracted from their tasks by the men in their lives. To her the only thing that mattered was making a success out of the business. Even if she thought Mr. Clay was a handsome man, there wasn't time for dalliances.

"Well, I think you should just ignore this stranger. Time is going to be flying by, Maggie, and before you know it your dance hall is going to be full of patrons."

"I can't very well ignore him, Lydia, not when I'm going to be seeing him every day."

"Then I trust you'll just learn to get along with him."

"From what I can tell he's nothing more than a pompous dandified man."

Thoughtfully, Maggie rose from the chair and walked with Lydia to the front door. "I don't wish to cause undue stress for Aunt Margaret. She seems to be getting better. The headaches come less frequently and her coloring has been good. And she is making more and more appearances in town these days."

"These are good signs, Maggie. They mean that our being here has helped her get better."

"Whatever the reason, let's hope her good health keeps up."

"Indeed." Giving her a quick hug, Maggie headed back to town, planning to stop by the mercantile to buy the material Lydia suggested.

Flicking the stub of the cigar on the ground, Sam squashed the remaining ember out with the toe of his boot. Then tugging the bottom of his vest into place, he continued to meander down Main Street. Mothers with their children in tow bustled along the walkways going about their errands.

The rainstorm that had plagued the region earlier today was long gone. Bright sunshine and blue skies had replaced the dark clouds. He was so busy admiring the crystalline skies that he wasn't watching where he was going and bumped right into a woman.

"Excuse me, ma'am. I apologize." Reaching out he caught her arm to steady her.

Looking into the woman's eyes it would have been hard to miss the sharp stare being returned.

Giving a slight bow, he said, "Why, Miss Maggie Monroe, please forgive my clumsiness. I'm afraid I was so caught up in looking at the scenery of your lovely little town that I wasn't watching where I was going."

"Please, let go of my hand, sir."

Ever so slowly he let her fingertips slip from his hand, enjoying the blush spreading over her face. "I was just heading to the post office to collect some items that I had shipped here."

If the train containing his two trunks had been on time, his belongings should be ready and waiting for him to pick up. He hoped so because he was more than ready to change out of the clothing he'd been in for the past two days.

"Might I suggest that you hurry along. The postmaster usually closes for the lunch hour."

Her comment brought a smile to his lips. "Are you trying to get rid of me, Miss Monroe?" Pulling his watch out of his vest pocket he flipped open the lid. "It's not even close to noontime yet." Snapping it shut, he returned the watch to its pocket.

"Oh for pity's sake, move out of my way. I

prefer not to waste my time lollygagging about when I've better things to be doing."

Putting on a sad face, he said, "Why, you wound me with your harsh words."

Rolling her eyes, she looked up at him. "Mr. Clay, I can see that you're not in the least bit wounded, now please let me go on with my business."

Stepping aside he let her pass by. This woman sure had some spunk in her and he had to say that he didn't mind that one little bit. He watched as she hoisted her skirts up to her attractive ankles and climbed the three steps leading to the mercantile. The bell above the door made a tinny sound as she went inside.

Pausing in front of the window, Sam contemplated the wisdom of following her. While doing so he caught sight of his reflection. A stylish bowler hat topped his blond hair and his neatly trimmed muttonchops defined the smooth planes of his face. Even dressed in day old travel worn clothing he still looked better than his father had on his best day.

When Samuel had struck out on his own over two years ago he didn't fathom the vastness of this country. And he hadn't regretted one minute of his life since then. He'd traveled up and down the East Coast by rail, in a stagecoach, and on horseback. He'd eaten in some of the finest restaurants this side of the Mississippi.

He'd more or less wasted the time away managing to grab a saloon job here or there. And now he had to make a go of his life here in Surprise or else he'd be back to farming the land. This little town had a great deal of potential. Surprise had nearly tripled its population in less than a year. This town was brought back from the brink of extinction.

Because of the rarity of this occurrence, the town had been featured in several of the larger newspaper publications. Sam saw immense opportunity for the right businessman. The advertisement in the paper had spoken to him almost as if it had been placed there for his eyes only.

He was a perfect fit for the job of manager of a dance hall. Apparently Margaret Monroe Sinclair had thought so too. She'd barely spoken to him and then hired him right on the spot, saying he was the perfect match for Maggie.

Sam had pondered her choice of words then, thinking she meant something more romantic, but then he realized that Miss Sinclair only meant he'd be perfect for the job.

He was about to move away from the window when he saw Maggie. She was standing in between a row of dry goods and sewing notions intently studying two bolts of fabric. From the frown on her face it appeared she was having trouble deciding on the right one.

Sam walked over to the door and pulled it open.

Chapter Four

Scents of rose oil, spices, and dry goods hit him all at once.

"Oooh! Mr. Jules, can you help me? I can't seem to decide which of these fabrics would be right for the dance hall."

Shaking his head, Sam walked over to where Miss Monroe stood wearing a perplexed look on her face. Fingering the pale muslin and then the softer cotton bolt, he said, "Neither one of these will do."

Shock registered on her face. "I don't believe I asked for your opinion."

He chuckled at her sarcasm.

"And I'm quite sure you didn't come in here to help me choose fabric. I thought you needed to get to the post office."

Leaning against a shelf that held stacks of blue chambray shirts and denim pants, he grinned. "Actually, I decided that could wait. I saw you from the window and knew right away that you were a lady needing my assistance."

Huffing out a breath, she muttered, "How charming. I don't need your help. As a matter of fact, I'm quite capable of handling this by myself."

With those words she hefted the muslin onto a table lined with bolts of brightly colored fabric and stalked off with the cotton cradled in her arms. "Mr. Jules!" she called out to the back of the store. "I'm ready with my purchases."

Spotting a shiny yellow bundle of material compelled him to do something he never would have done if she hadn't presented a challenge to him by deliberately snubbing him.

"Wait!" Grabbing the fabric, he practically raced to the counter ahead of her. Slapping the material on the counter, he smiled. "This will be much better."

"You don't even know what I'm buying this for."

"I was hoping you'd be having some hostess gowns made." He beamed his most charming smile at her.

Light brown eyebrows shot up and her face turned beet red. "I think your assumptions are a bit personal."

It occurred to him then, as it so often did, too late, that he may have just overstepped the boundaries. Offering up fashion advice to a woman he'd just met was probably not the best thing to be doing, leastwise not until he was on better terms with her.

"Let me guess—curtains, tablecloths?" he quickly changed tactics, continuing to badger her.

Pushing aside his choice, she made room for hers. "If you must know I'm having some draperies made for the front windows."

Picking at the filmy material, he grimaced. A plain, puritan choice for a plain woman, he thought. And then he looked at Miss Monroe. Her face was flushed; he didn't know if it was in anger or what he supposed was her frustration at having to deal with him yet again today. Her blue eyes flashed and her hands trembled ever so slightly.

He realized with a start that there was nothing puritan about her. He'd seen something spark within her. Then just as quickly she'd gathered her wits about her.

"Mr. Clay, I'd thank you not to offer your opinion about my purchases again. For that matter, please don't trouble yourself over the dance hall either."

A short thin man with dark hair and spectacles perched high on his thin nose came out from behind the curtained doorway. Samuel assumed this was the owner of the mercantile.

"Is this man bothering you, Miss Maggie?"

Sliding a sly look in his general direction, she replied, "Everything is fine, Mr. Jules."

Noticing the hefty bolt of fabric, he said, "I see you found what you were looking for."

Sticking his hand out, Sam introduced himself. "I'm new to town. Samuel Clay's my name and I was just hired by Margaret Monroe Sinclair to manage the dance hall."

Looking doubtfully from Maggie to Mr. Clay, Mr. Jules frowned. "A manager for the dance hall? That should help things along don't you think, Miss Maggie?"

"Apparently, what I think is of no consequence anymore. If you don't mind, please have this delivered to the seamstress, Mrs. Waring. She'll be expecting it this afternoon."

"I'll see that it gets done," Mr. Jules replied, taking the bolt of fabric off the counter.

Maggie left the store and walked out into the heat of the day. Within minutes, sweat formed along her hairline and moisture gathered between her shoulder blades, making her wonder, as she often did, how it could be so humid in such a mountainous region. With the craggy peaks and valleys of the Catskills surrounding the town one would think that there would always be cool breezes. Well, such was not the case on this particular afternoon.

The brief rainstorm, which had moved through hours ago, left in its wake soggy air, the kind that caused moss to grow under the big boulders found along the edges of the town.

Pushing a damp strand of hair off her forehead, she stewed over Samuel Clay. The pesky man kept turning up. He was smug, self-assured, and well dressed. She felt he came off as a bit overdressed and somewhat overzealous. Walking about in those black dress pants, a crisp white shirt, and the most brilliant vest she'd ever laid eyes upon.

The audacity of him to even suggest what she should be wearing. Of course, the sad truth was she would be in need of some new gowns. But why oh why did he have to be the one to point that out to her? Mentally she added that to the growing list of things to be done.

Walking along the street, Maggie had to step around more than one group of loiterers. The place was booming compared to what it had been when she'd first arrived here months ago. It was hard to believe that almost a full year had gone by.

Abigail and now Lydia had both found the man of their dreams and had married him. Abby was still the sheriff and Lydia the schoolteacher. Who would have guessed those two would have settled into such fine, stable lives? She couldn't help but think, *and then there was one.*

She knew her future lay in making the dance hall a successful business venture. Under her steady hand it would be done. Aunt Margaret had entrusted her with this challenge and she was more than ready for it. In fact Maggie relished the challenge. She had her plan in place.

Maggie liked to think that the woman she'd been named for, Margaret Monroe Sinclair, her aunt, understood this. Maybe she did, perhaps she didn't. Nonetheless, Maggie was going to be a successful, independent woman and no one was going to deter her.

* * *

Margaret Monroe Sinclair stood at her bedroom window. The hustle and bustle of the new Surprise stunned even her, surpassing her modest expectations. She was delighted to see wagons carrying supplies into town, as well as buggies with families. There was even talk of putting a stagecoach stop here in addition to the train depot. Who could have guessed that one well placed advertisement in a city newspaper would have caused such change in one small town?

With a steady hand, she pushed back an errant strand of her thinning gray hair. Sighing, she realized that for the first time in a long time she was truly content. Her town—the one she and her husband had founded more than thirty years ago—was alive and prospering. What more could an old woman hope for?

There was the small matter of seeing her three precious nieces happy, she thought reflectively. That goal had fallen a little short with Maggie, the last one to be wed. She was so busy with the dance hall Margaret feared that if a man were to drop from heaven and land at her feet she'd give him no notice. She'd probably step right over him and continue on with her work.

Maggie was stubborn, she'd give her that. This could be a good trait, but not in the matter of men. Margaret feared there would never be a man suitable for her last unmarried niece.

Where Maggie was concerned, the match had to be with someone extraordinary. Looking out the window, she found herself searching the streets for the man. He was out there, she'd made certain of it.

Chapter Five

A week after his arrival, Sam had managed to secure his room at Mrs. Bartholomew's boarding house indefinitely. Today he was waiting at the telegraph office for a response to a message he'd sent out two days ago. Tapping his toe impatiently, he waited.

"I don't see anything here, Mr. Clay."

"Why that's impossible, kind sir. There should be something." Pointing to the small pile of paper, Sam said, "Check again."

Doing as he was told, the small, rotund man with dark hair and a protruding nose shuffled through the stack. "Nothing, sir, I'm sorry. Come back this afternoon, there might be something in by then." With that the man dismissed him, turning back to his work.

Before he'd left Albany, Sam had happened upon a new dance troupe and he thought the hall would be the perfect venue for them. Hoping to hire them before they were completely booked, Sam had sent a message off yesterday. If he didn't hear from them soon there would be no other choice except to find a replacement.

Snapping his fingers, he left the telegraph office and stepped out into the bright sunshine, squinting his eyes against the sudden glare. Like a little boy with time on his hands, he glanced mischievously up and down Main Street.

There must be something he could do to pass the time while he waited for the response.

"Maggie, how many times have I got to tell you that you can't change the color of the paint once it's been picked out?"

"Must you yell so everyone can hear, Cole?"

"That's it. I don't care how much Abby begs me, I'm not going to put up with your stubbornness another minute. I have other customers to deal with, not just you, you know!"

Sam turned to where Miss Maggie and her cousin's husband were having a standoff. The back of the buckboard they were leaning against was filled with buckets of paint, drop cloths, and brushes. Parked in front of the Judson Lumber Company, it looked loaded and ready to be transported across the street to the dance hall.

Color rode high on her cheeks and Cole looked about ready to explode. Hands fisted at his sides, he towered over the young woman. This fact didn't seem to bother her one bit.

Standing toe to toe with him, she leaned close to his face. "I don't think this is the right shade of green for the stage floor. And furthermore, this is not the color I chose."

"Samuel ordered the paint earlier this week. I assumed he'd discussed the decision with you."

"He most certainly did not!" Maggie huffed.

As if sensing his nearness, she turned on him. "You! Get over here right this instant!"

Now most things didn't frighten Samuel, but the look on her face almost sent him running back into the telegraph office. Instead, taking a deep fortifying breath, he exhaled slowly while walking over to her.

He was within three feet of her before she pounced.

"I am not going to use this color on the stage, Mr. Clay."

"I don't care. It's what you're stuck with, Miss Maggie. You're already so far over budget with supplies that I don't think Miss Margaret is going to stand for any more of your work order changes."

Even from where he stood, Sam was sure he heard her teeth grinding together.

Through a clenched jaw, she said, "I'll deal with Aunt Margaret."

"I'm afraid that you're going to have to deal with me. And I'm not changing the paint. It's as simple as that. You either take this order or the floors will be bare." Folding his arms across his chest, Samuel glared down at her.

"I am not taking that paint, Samuel Clay. As far as I'm concerned you can paint the entire town with this hideous shade of green." With that she flounced off, leaving the men to stare after her open-mouthed.

Draping his arms over the side of the wagon, Sam drawled, "Good day, Mr. Stanton."

"It was until she came along." He pointed at Maggie's back.

"She sure is strong-willed," Sam commented.

"You can say that again."

Toying with the top of one of the buckets, Sam kept an eye on Miss Maggie who was now on the other side of the street speaking to a redheaded woman. She was nodding at something Miss Maggie was saying as she gesticulated in the general direction of the lumber company.

The redhead was nodding sympathetically, while a taller woman with long dark hair wearing a sheriff's star pinned to the front of her blouse joined them.

"Oh, shoot." Throwing his hands in the air, Stanton began to backtrack toward the doorway of the building behind them.

"Now she's going to involve both of her cousins in this argument and before you know it the whole day will have been spent smoothing down their ruffled feathers."

Frowning at the trio of women, Sam said, "Since it's me she's mad at, I'll go talk to them. I'm sure Miss Monroe can be persuaded to take the paint."

Stopping, he turned to look at Sam, his eyes narrowed. "You sure you want to do something so dangerous?"

Shrugging his shoulders, he looked at Mr. Stanton and smiled. "Why not? I've got a few hours to kill."

"She's all yours." Cole stalked away, leaving Sam to face Miss Maggie Monroe in all her fury.

"Where's Cole off to?" she snapped, rushing toward him.

"Guess he had some work to do."

"I'm still not taking this paint."

Holding his hands out like a peace offering,

Sam said, "Look, it's a great deal of paint. It would be a sinful waste of our precious resources to let the paint go to waste." Flashing her his most charming smile, he figured he'd won the argument.

She appeared to be pondering this. Her arms were neatly folded across her chest and her baby blue eyes were narrowed in concentration. "You're right about that. It would be a terrible waste of time and money."

"Is it too dark or too light?" he asked, curious as to her reason for rejecting the color.

"It's too bright. I was thinking more of a forest green. You know, a deep, rich color, not this unsightly lime green *you* came up with."

"The color will work on the stage. When the only thing lighting the area during a performance will be lanterns and candlelight from the chandeliers, the color will appear duller."

"I still don't like it."

"You've no other choice, Miss, except to use this paint."

"Fine. I still hate the color and I hate it even more that you're bullying me."

He laughed at her, which only seemed to irk her more. "I'm not a bully, Miss Monroe. I'm just doing the job your aunt is paying me to do."

"And there's another thing—she hired you

without even consulting with me. I'd like to know what makes you so qualified for the job."

"I've worked in the business before. Perhaps she thought my experience would be helpful in making this venture as successful as possible."

"I don't think so."

"Well, it's neither here nor there. The stage will be painted by the end of this week. I trust you to oversee the work."

"Where are you going to be?"

"I have some business to attend to that may take me out of town for a day or two." His desire to have the dance troupe booked for the hall was so great that he'd decided rather than waiting for the telegram which might never come, he'd go back to Albany and personally convince them to come here.

She looked to be mulling this over and then a sudden smile illuminated her face. Sam didn't like the looks of it, either. He had a sixth sense when it came to women and their hijinks. And he could tell from the twinkle in her eyes that Miss Maggie was definitely up to something.

"All right, Mr. Clay. You can trust me to see that the job gets done properly."

"Now that's been settled, let's go inside and see where we're at with everything else."

Turning, she walked in the direction of the hall

with Sam close behind. Entering the cool room he was satisfied with the changes.

The bar area had been sanded and refinished. Neat rows of tall iced tea glasses lined the flat surface in front of it. On the opposite side were several dozen teapots with gold-rimmed cups and saucers next to them.

A row of tall stools lined the front of the bar. Each was covered with a tufted cushion. Wandering behind the bar, Sam saw there was a space for kegs of root beer and sarsaparilla. Unlike the halls he frequented, he knew that Miss Maggie wasn't going to be serving alcoholic beverages. Sam wasn't sure how this would be for the business, but he suspected they'd know soon enough.

After the fight over the paint color he wasn't about to bring up the prospect of serving such libations in this establishment.

"The draperies and tablecloths will be ready by the end of the week." Turning around to face him, she added, "Just a few more finishing touches and then we'll be open for business."

He saw the flicker of worry puckering her brow. "Is there a problem?"

"Not really. I haven't been able to settle on all of the entertainment. The manual says you need to have a dance instructor."

Laughter erupted from him and Maggie desired nothing more than to wrap her hands around his neck and strangle him. She didn't see what was so funny. With hands on her hips, she advanced on him.

"What is so funny, Mr. Clay?"

"You are. I have to tell you, I've been in this business a very long time and never have I had to hire a dance instructor."

"I don't care what you did in the past, Mr. Clay. This is my hall and I'm going to run it the correct way. You probably had floozies and the like running around your establishment."

"I daresay I did not have any such women running my place."

He seemed to be truly insulted by her remark so Maggie tried again. "I want the patrons to be able to have a good time and having someone here to teach them the proper moves would . . ." she frowned while searching for the right word, "enhance their experience."

That sent him to laughing once more and Maggie felt the hackles on her neck raise in anger. "You should just leave, go someplace else! Find another hall to run because I don't need you here!"

Spreading his arms wide, he looked at her. "Trust me on this. People who come here are not looking for instruction, they are looking to have a good time."

"Well, I disagree with you. I think there are those who would like to learn the latest dances and not have to look foolish while doing it."

His raised his eyebrows suddenly. "You don't know how to dance."

It wasn't a question, but a statement and he made it sound as if she had the plague. Lying had never come easy to her, so, shrugging her shoulders, Maggie decided to ignore the comment. Taking the dreaded book off the corner of the bar, she secreted it away in her pocket. Then she wandered over to the stage area, picturing in her mind how it would look a week from now.

The candles would all be lit casting a warm glow over the entire room. The three-piece orchestra would be set up off to the right and a few small tables would fill the floor in front around them. She could envision the dancers on the stage spinning and waltzing for the audience.

It was going to be so elegant. And no one—not her aunt and certainly not Samuel Clay—was going to spoil this for her. Maggie turned to look at the man and found him standing in front of the stage with his feet spread apart and his arms folded across his chest.

Tipping his head to one side, he looked at her curiously.

"What?" she spat the word out.

"A dance hall hostess who doesn't know how to dance, how interesting."

Sucking in her lower lip, Maggie fumed. Sliding her hand into her skirt pocket, she did her best to hide the pages of the manual. She planned on practicing later when he was gone.

Taking a step toward her, he said, "I can teach you."

Chapter Six

"I don't think that would be a good idea." She backed away from him.

"Why not?"

"We barely like each other, Mr. Clay. I don't see the two of us as dance partners."

He put his hand over his heart and she knew he was about to tell her how her words had wounded him. Before he could say it, she raised her hand, stopping him from speaking.

"Please don't tell me again how much I wound you."

Lowering his hand, he smiled at her. Not a put-on, made-up smile like that kind he enjoyed using to charm her, but a genuine smile that started beneath his moustache at the corners of his mouth and reached all the way up to his blue-green eyes.

She felt her reserve slipping. She planned on using the manual for her pretend partner, but having a flesh and blood male one *would* be better. Her fingers released the pages of the book.

"You have to promise me that no one else will know about this."

"I can do that." Taking off his jacket, he draped it over a chair in the corner.

"There is one other favor I must ask of you, Mr. Clay."

"And what might that be?"

"I want you to be yourself. No sarcastic remarks or false smiles."

Maggie was tired of constantly being required to have her guard up around him. It was exhausting trying to keep up with his quick-witted remarks and she wanted to be able to concentrate on the steps he was going to teach her.

His face became serious and Maggie waited for the retort sure to follow. "I will try to behave myself. And you, Miss Maggie, will try to have some fun!"

"Fun!" she had barely squeaked the word out when he took her in his arms.

The book fell from her pocket onto the floor. Bending over, Samuel picked up the dog-eared copy of *Mr. Boxer's Dancing Tutorial.* Raising one eyebrow he looked at her. His mouth opened and then snapped shut. Very carefully he placed it on the edge of the stage.

"We won't be needing this."

Returning to her side he placed one hand lightly on her waist and took her other hand in his. "We'll start with a basic waltz. It's very simple, just follow my steps, one-two-three."

Blinking up at him, she could see his pulse beating at the side of his neck. Taking a deep breath she caught the scent of his masculinity and her stomach did the strangest flip-flop.

Maggie whispered, "The manual instructions specifically say that the man and woman should be a ruler's length apart. I think we're too close, Mr. Clay."

Pulling away from him, she concentrated on putting the proper amount of space between them. She thought that when their arms were stretched out and when their hands were barely touching was good enough.

Laughter spilled from his lips. "Miss Maggie, the book said a ruler's length, not a yardstick." With a gentle tug he managed to pull her back into his arms. "Now, come on, we're going to waltz. Just make a box with your steps."

Coaxing her, Samuel swept them around the space in front of the stage. The first steps were awkward and surely painful for him. She stepped on the poor man's toes four times. Frustrated, she pulled them to a stop.

"This isn't going to work. I simply have two left feet!"

Quirking an eyebrow at her, he said, "Maggie Monroe, are you giving up?"

She shook her head.

"The first problem is that you're as stiff as a board."

"I am not," she defended herself.

"Yes, you are. Now take a deep breath and relax. Then I want you to stop concentrating on the steps and do what feels natural."

Slowly they started moving and this time he hummed a simple waltz tune. It was much easier when there was music accompanying the steps. Maggie felt herself relaxing. She even managed a smile.

"Where did you learn how to dance?"

"My mother taught me. We didn't have much entertainment around, so we had to invent our own fun. During the summer when the evening air was warm enough to be outside on the porch, my father would play his violin while my mother taught me simple dance steps."

Subtly he broadened their steps, moving them into the middle of the room.

"That's a very nice memory," she said wistfully. "How come you never learned how to dance before this?"

Shrugging, she replied, "I don't know. I suppose it didn't really interest me all that much."

He slowed their pace. "And now?"

He was looking down at her and she got lost in the serious expression on his face. It was rare when he showed his true self. There was something reflected in his gaze that she couldn't quite put a name to. He was looking at her like a man would look at a woman he found attractive. But in her heart she knew it couldn't be so; they barely even liked each other, did they?

It was a few minutes before Maggie realized they'd stopped moving. He'd rearranged his position, letting his hands rest on her waistline.

"Now, I find dancing very intriguing."

"Good. At our next lesson I'll introduce you to a reel."

Stepping away from him, Maggie watched him walk over to the chair where he'd left his coat. Whatever warmth she'd experience just moments before was gone.

He appeared to be lost in thought. And Maggie was surprised to find that her arms felt empty. Her thoughts were spinning around in her head all topsy-turvy. In just a short span of time she'd felt her disposition toward him softening a bit. She watched him turn to face her and realized with a start he was wearing the same cocky, devil-may-care smile he always wore.

She stared at him from across the room, amazed at how quickly he'd transformed into his old self. He acted like a man full of self-confidence and with a purpose to life. Frankly, Maggie thought as she did before the lesson that he was just full of himself. And if she had a type of man, one she might find attractive, she tried hard to tell herself Samuel Clay wouldn't be the one at all.

And yet there was something about him.

He moved away from the window so suddenly that Maggie took a step backward.

"I have some business to take care of. Oh, and don't forget to take care of the painting." Abruptly he left the building, leaving Maggie standing there with her mouth open wondering what he was up to.

Not about to let him leave so easily she followed him to the doorway. “Wait, when is our next lesson going to be?”

Looking over his shoulder at her, he said with a wink, “When I get back.”

Chapter Seven

The next morning Maggie awoke to a brilliant Catskill Mountain day filled with sunshine and the sweet scent of honeysuckle. Before going to bed the night before, she'd made a list of all the things to be done today.

Right at the top she had written "paint the stage." Still fuming about the color, Maggie threw back the coverlet and climbed out of bed. She was going to show Mr. Clay who was boss. Pulling a simple brown dress over her head, she worked nimble fingers buttoning up the front.

Opening the bedroom door, Maggie's senses were teased with the scent of Anna's famous blueberry scones. Her mouth watering in anticipation, Maggie went downstairs to the breakfast room.

Entering the room she found Aunt Margaret seated on one side of the oval table. "Good morning, Aunt Margaret! What a pleasant surprise this is."

"Good morning, Maggie. I woke up this morning feeling quite chipper so I decided to come down for breakfast."

Pulling out one of the chintz-covered chairs, Maggie sat. "I'm glad you did. It will give us a chance to catch up."

Sipping from her teacup, Aunt Margaret peered at her over the rim. "So tell me, how are you and Mr. Clay getting along?"

Swallowing the first bite of scone, Maggie said, "As well as can be expected." Thinking about yesterday's lessons she thought they were getting along better than she expected.

Still, the man had little nuances that annoyed her. "He's quite set in his ways. Did you know this when you hired him?"

A wisp of graying hair fell across her cheek as she shook her head. "I knew he had a great deal of experience in running an enterprise such as this one."

"That's all well and good, but what do you

really know about this man? Do you know where he comes from? Does he have any family to speak of? Where did he live before coming to Surprise?" The questions that had been building up inside of her for days now came out in short bursts.

"Maggie, slow down. I can barely keep up." Leaning back in her chair, Aunt Margaret frowned thoughtfully.

The clock on the mantle chimed eight times. There was a great deal to be done today and if Maggie had any hopes of getting the painting done before Mr. Clay came back from wherever he'd wandered off to, she had to leave the house soon. But not before she got some answers from her aunt.

"Aunt Margaret? Do you know anything at all about him other than the fact that he can run a dance hall?"

"I know what my instincts tell me."

Rolling her eyes heavenward, Maggie suppressed the urge to yell. She dearly loved this woman, but there were times, like right this minute, when she was so exasperating Maggie didn't know what to do with her.

Laying her napkin alongside the breakfast plate, Maggie pushed away from the table. "Let's hope your instincts aren't wrong."

As she was leaving the room Maggie could have sworn that she heard her aunt say, "They never are."

Going down the slate walkway in front of the house, Maggie spotted Mrs. Bartholomew hanging bed linens out on a clothesline stretching from one corner of her house to a tree behind it. The freshly laundered sheets snapped and fluttered in the warm morning breeze.

After waiting for a wagon loaded with lumber to rattle by her, Maggie walked over to the boarding house with a single purpose in mind—to find out exactly where Mr. Clay was.

"Good morning, Mrs. Bartholomew."

"Morning, Maggie. How is Margaret faring?"

Brushing at the front of her dress where a bee had landed, Maggie replied, "She's doing quite well. I think the worst of her health crisis has passed."

Bending over, the owner of the boarding house plucked another sheet from the wicker basket. Shaking it free of the damp wrinkles, she gathered a handful of clothespins and hung it on the line.

For the briefest of moments Maggie found herself wondering if those sheets were the ones Mr. Clay slept on. Giving a quick shake of her head, she brought herself back to the reason she was here.

"Do you have a full house now?"

"As a matter of fact, with Mr. Clay here, all of my rooms are taken." Smiling broadly at her, the woman added, "Isn't it wonderful the way the town is prospering?"

Maggie only nodded in reply while the woman chattered on.

"I daresay I'm going to have to hire some extra help if this keeps up. I can barely make it through a day with just one helper as it is."

"I'm glad things are going well for you, Mrs. Bartholomew." Running her hands over the tips of a small patch of daisies growing alongside the house, she inquired as innocently as possible, "Is Mr. Clay back from his trip yet?"

"I don't believe he will be back until day after tomorrow."

Maggie raised her eyebrows in surprise. She didn't know he'd be gone so long. But better for her that he was. There were things to be tended to and it would be best if he weren't around interfering.

"Well, I must be going. Have a good day."

"You too, dear."

As Maggie made her way to the hall, she had time to think about what she was going to do with the hideous paint. The matter of the color still rankled her, causing her not one, but two sleepless nights. Maybe the color choice didn't seem important to Mr. Clay, but to Maggie it mattered a great deal.

When the dance hall of Surprise opened next week she didn't want one thing to be out of place. The building from the rooftop right down to the foundation had to be perfect. Pausing outside the doorway she looked up at the front of the building. Tapping her finger lightly against her lower lip she considered the problem of the paint.

She hit upon the idea just as the sunlight poured through the gap in the tree line striking the white clapboards. Rushing across the street she found Alexander inside the mill.

"Hello, Alexander."

Nodding, he said, "Good day to you, Maggie. What can I do for you?"

It never ceased to amaze her how he was always all business and she wondered, as she had so many times before, what her cousin Lydia found so exciting about the man.

Be that as it may, she had a lot to accomplish before the egotistical Samuel Clay came back. "Alexander, I could use your help. I need to get some painting done and I'd really like to have it finished before Mr. Clay comes back. I was wondering if you might have a worker or two you could spare for the day."

"I just hired on two of Walter Smith's sons. I can send them over right now."

"That would be wonderful. Thank you, Alexander."

Feeling her day brighten immensely, she hummed a little ditty as she crossed the street with the two boys trailing after her. With paintbrushes in their hands, they seemed eager to get to work.

Bringing them to a halt in front of the building, she turned and smiled. "Here is what I want you to paint." Quickly she explained the plan to them, instructed them on where they could find the buckets of paint, and went inside.

At noontime she poked her head out the door to offer the young men some lunch and tall glasses of lemonade. After eating and drinking their fill they went back to work. By the time the sun was beginning to dip low in the sky they were finished with the painting job.

Stepping out in the street a bit, Maggie couldn't hide her grimace of distaste. It was perfect. She could hardly wait for Mr. Clay to come back to see his reaction to her creative use of the ugly green paint.

* * *

By the time Sam arrived back in Surprise it was nearing midnight. Letting himself into the boarding house by way of the back door, he crept up the stairs to his room. Divesting himself of his dust-laden clothing, he lay facedown on the featherbed and fell sound asleep.

Bright sunlight poured through the window waking him with a jolt. For a moment he couldn't remember where he was, but quickly realized he was back in Surprise. He lay there for a few minutes listening to the sounds of morning, remembering the way it felt to have Maggie dancing in his arms. Sam had been shaken by his reaction to her.

His sole intention had been to teach her the simplest of waltz steps, not on developing any kind of attraction to her. He'd been glad for the reprieve of taking care of business away from this town. It had given him some much needed time to get his thoughts about the woman straight.

The creak of a wagon wheel as it rolled along the gravelly street, the gleeful laughter of children as they romped in backyards, a bird twittering just outside his window, and the clanging of pots from the kitchen downstairs, all signaled to Sam that the town was awakening.

Groaning, he rolled onto his back. Throwing

his legs over the side of the bed, Sam reluctantly got up to start the day. A vision of a certain blond-haired, blue-eyed young woman flitted through his mind. He wondered how Miss Maggie had spent her time while he was gone.

Smiling just a little, Sam proceeded with his morning ritual of shaving, dressing, and lastly applying a liberal dose of pomade to his hair. Smoothing the last of his thick locks in place, he wiped his hands on a towel. After adjusting his vest, he left the room.

Descending the stairs he was greeted by the smells of crisp bacon, eggs, and toasted bread.

"Morning, Mrs. Bartholomew."

Turning from the stove, where she'd been busy scrambling the eggs in a hot, cast-iron pan, she looked at him in surprise.

"Why, Mr. Clay, I didn't hear you come in."

"Didn't mean to startle you, ma'am. I got back late last night and let myself in the back door."

"I thought I heard that top stair creak a bit last night. Thought it was my tabby cat."

"Nope, it was just me."

"Sit," she ordered. "I'm just finishing up these eggs."

Pulling a chair out from the end of the long planked table that filled the center of the room,

Sam sat. "So, anything interesting happen while I was gone?"

Her back to him, she answered, "Not that I'm aware of. Miss Maggie stopped by wondering when you were coming back."

Sam's eyebrows rose in speculation of why Maggie had done such a thing.

"I think she missed you."

Chuckling at the thought, Sam accepted the plate of bacon and eggs that Mrs. Bartholomew held out to him. "Now *that* I seriously doubt."

"Well, she seemed mighty interested in your whereabouts."

He'd just bet she did. One thing he'd learned in a hurry was that Maggie Monroe didn't like being left out. He imagined his leaving town under such secrecy bothered her a great deal. The thought left him smiling as he finished his breakfast.

Grabbing his hat off the rack by the back door, Sam said, "Have a good day, Mrs. Bartholomew."

"You too, Mr. Clay."

Whistling, Sam fairly swaggered down the street to the dance hall. He was feeling like the world was his oyster this morning. And so it should be. His little trip out of town proved very fruitful and he couldn't wait to share his news with Maggie.

Suddenly he stood still. With his mouth hanging open, he stared at the dance hall. What had she done?

He was going to strangle her!

The paint that he'd purchased for the stage now adorned the trim surrounding all of the windows. The bright green color shined like an unwelcome beacon against the white clapboards.

"Maggie!" Anger pulsed through him as he raced through the swinging doors into the center of the hall. "Where is she?" he shouted.

Chapter Eight

He saw her kneeling on the floor of the stage area. Her back was to him, affording him an unobstructed view of one very curvaceous rump. If the sight of her in such a pose hadn't stopped him dead in his tracks, rendering him speechless, Samuel would have let her have it. As it was he could barely speak. His next breath had caught somewhere between his lungs and his throat.

Coughing and sputtering like an idiot, he made his way toward her. He found it hard to believe she hadn't heard him shouting. It was quite evident he was being ignored. Considering himself a man to be reckoned with, his stride lengthened, closing the distance between them to a few steps.

"Maggie! I know you heard me shouting." He so wanted to reach out and swat her backside.

Calmly, as if nothing out of the ordinary had transpired, she turned, tucking her legs underneath her as she sat on the stage floor facing him. Blue eyes framed by long, blond lashes looked up at him.

"Mr. Clay. You're back. I didn't hear you come in."

Advancing on her, he said, "Don't get sarcastic with me, Missy."

"Don't call me 'Missy'."

"Maggie." He amended. "Don't pretend like you didn't hear me yelling."

"Oh, was that you? I didn't recognize the voice. So tell me, what has you so upset you had to yell?"

"You know darn well why I was yelling!" Turning slightly, he pointed toward the doorway. "That paint, you put the paint which I had intended for the stage area on the outside of the building."

"Yes. I did. Don't you think it looks lovely?"

"No."

Getting to her feet, Maggie towered above him from the stage. "I distinctly remember what you said the day you came into town."

Now that comment struck a cord in him. He'd said a lot of things his first day in Surprise. Placing his hands on his hips so he wasn't tempted to reach out and strangle her, he said, "Go on."

"You were talking about the blandness of the sign and mentioned something about how I didn't have any taste when it came to colors." Sauntering across the stage, she continued her little speech. "You also said people would need to be attracted to the outside of the building if they were expected to patronize this establishment."

He noticed for the first time that she was wearing her hair in a single braid that fell down her back, skimming her waist. Sam hadn't realized her hair was so long. He wondered what it would feel like sliding through his fingers.

She turned and began pacing back across the stage. Her dark blue dress was buttoned right up to her neck despite the warm, humid air. He found himself wishing she would reach up and undo a few of the flat black buttons. He imagined the skin against her throat to be lily white and soft as a petal to the touch.

"And it was you who stated the color had to be used because I was already over budget. So you see, Mr. Clay, I think it was thrifty of me and a bit creative to use the paint on the outside window trim. Don't you agree?" Kneeling in front of him so they were eye to eye, she smiled.

Feeling a tad bit flustered under her careful scrutiny, he took a step back. Clearing his throat as well as his mind he said, "The paint was for the stage. It would have worked quite well there."

"What's done is done, as they say." Slapping her hands together she stood up and came down the steps leading from the stage to the main floor.

Her scent of lilacs floated around him. If he didn't know any better, he'd think she was deliberately trying to distract him by using her feminine wiles. But this was, after all, Maggie Monroe, stiff, staid, and almost prudish in her demeanor. A woman who, he was quickly learning, didn't waste time on idle flirtations and was all business and no fun.

Turning, he followed her with his gaze. In his haste to find her, he hadn't even noticed that the room was set up. Small, intimate, round tables edged the dance floor with four white, wrought iron chairs encircling each one.

Soft yellow cloths covered each tabletop and in the center was a miniature kerosene lantern. His gaze continued around the hall as he took note of the filmy white curtains that had been hung from each of the tall windows flanking the entryway. The material fluttered as a breeze wafted through, bringing with it the tangy scent of freshly cut hay.

All in all, the place was shaping up better than he'd hoped. They would be ready for the grand opening two nights from now. His trip to Albany had proven more fruitful than he could have hoped for. The surprise he had planned for Miss Maggie was set to arrive late Friday afternoon.

Right now his only thought was to get back in the good graces of Maggie. Strolling over to where she stood behind the oak bar, he leaned an elbow on the polished slab. "I like what you've done with the place."

Her back still to him, she replied, her tone matter of fact, "Thank you. I found putting everything in place went much easier without any distractions."

"You think I'm a distraction?"

Turning around, she looked at him. He had to squash a grin when he detected the hint of a blush across her cheeks. Obviously he'd hit a nerve with the question.

Rolling back her shoulders, she sighed. "Well, I must admit, you really are a bit of one, always looking over my shoulder, double-checking my work."

He shrugged. "Tell you what—just for you I will try to amend my ways."

Nibbling on her lower lip, she appeared to be mulling this over. "You could start by telling me where you were for the past two days."

Finding it interesting that she cared at all about his whereabouts, Sam answered, "I had some business to take care of."

"Did it have to do with the hall? Because if it did I need to know what it was."

Pulling up a stool, he sat. "You *need* to know?"

"Yes." Perching on a stool behind the bar, she sat across from him with her bent elbows on the surface, resting her chin on top of her folded hands. "Look, Mr. Clay, whether we like it or not, we're partners in this venture. I think it's high time we got to know each other a little better, don't you?"

A tingle of trepidation skittered down his spine. It was never good when a woman wanted to get to know you better. "All right, what would you like to know about me?"

"First off, where did you go the day before yesterday?"

"I went to Albany." Keep the answers as simple as possible, he thought. With time running out on the agreement he'd made with his father, Sam had booked the act which would be sure to bring fast revenue to their business.

"I see. And what did you do while you were there?"

"I checked on some of the entertainment." A little white lie never hurt anyone.

"You could have discussed this with me before leaving town in such a hurry."

Her tone was accusatory, and this time he allowed her those feelings. She was right; he should have spoken to her before he left, but the fact was he'd been disturbed by his reaction to her when they were dancing. He needed to put some distance between them. Lining up the entertainment she wasn't going to approve of anytime soon had done the trick.

"I'm sorry for not telling you what I was doing."

"Apology accepted."

Hang on a minute, a little voice inside his head warned, *she's giving in much too easily.*

"I'll make a deal with you, Mr. Clay. You get over being angry about my having the trim painted the hideous green color and I'll forgive you for going off to Albany without discussing it with me first."

He looked at her like she'd lost her mind. It wasn't any kind of a deal, leastwise not one he wanted to be making. The trim looked horrible and he wasn't about to give her all the details of his trip. Looking into her blue eyes, though, he could see from the cool gaze being returned there was no negotiating to be had.

For Maggie Monroe it was all or nothing.

Like in a poker game, Sam knew when the deck was stacked against him. And like any true gentleman, he knew when to fold. Extending his hand to her, he said, "You have a deal, Miss Monroe."

Her firm grip startled him and feeling as if they'd come to an understanding of sorts, he was reluctant to let her hand go. The fact was, he'd never thought of her as a vain woman and found that her skin felt silky smooth under his. It was hard for him to imagine her taking the time to apply lotions, but running his thumb lightly over hers, he was glad she did.

Seeing the blush creeping up over her face, he smiled. When she tried to pull her hand away, he couldn't resist toying with her. He held onto her hand for a moment longer before releasing her. "So, it looks like our little talk is finished."

Tipping her head to one side and narrowing her eyes, she said, "No, we're far from finished." Reaching under the bar, she set two tall glasses in front of them. "Let me pour you a sarsaparilla."

Chapter Nine

Ignoring the unexpected sensation of awareness running from the tips of her fingers up along her arms, Maggie concentrated on pouring the sarsaparilla. The man sitting on the other side of the bar—as loathe as she was to admit, if even to no one other than herself—intrigued her.

Placing the drink in front of him, she ran her finger around the rim of her glass. Deciding where to begin was posing quite the problem and he just sat there, staring at her. There was so much she wanted to find out about Samuel Clay. He was a fine dancer and had grown up on a farm, but she still didn't know much more about him than the day she'd first met him.

Deciding to get right to the point, Maggie asked, "Where are you from, Mr. Clay?"

"Excuse me?" He looked across the narrow bar at her, surprise at her question evident in his expression.

"Tell me about the farm you grew up on and your family." Not one to beat around the bush, she forged ahead with her little inquisition.

His Adam's apple bobbed as he gulped down a mouthful of drink. "You always need to know so much about a person?"

Pulling her mouth into a straight line, she thought he was being evasive. Now she really wanted to know more about him. "I don't know anything at all about you and well, you know most everything there is to know about me."

Winking at her, he said, "I hardly know *everything* about you, Miss Maggie."

Shrugging off the discomfort brought on by his warm gaze, she tried again. "What of your family, Mr. Clay?"

"There's my mother, father, and my one brother." As if anticipating what her next question would be, he added, "And they are all still living."

"Where do they live now?"

"They're still living on a farm in the northern part of the state."

Studying him more closely, Maggie thought

he certainly didn't look like any farmer she knew. His hands bore none of the hard calluses brought on by working long hours in the fields. Nor did his face bear any signs of wear from being outdoors day after day in all sorts of weather conditions.

"Is something wrong?" The smile faded from his hazel eyes as Mr. Clay stared back at her.

"Let's just say you don't bear the signs of having been a farmer."

"I didn't say I was one. I said my family lives on a farm. They are the farmers."

He looked annoyed now and she wondered why. Making a living from the land was what most people in these parts did. It was an honest way to make a living. If you didn't live in a town owning mercantile, lumberyards, and the like, then you provided for your family in the only other way available, which was farming.

"You make it sound like being a farmer is something to be ashamed of."

He squirmed on the stool. "Clearly you've never had to toil away hours on end in the rain, snow, and hot sun just to put food on the table. Not to mention the endless time spent planting a crop only to have it ruined by a hailstorm. You should be thankful you've been afforded the good life."

The unmistakable sound of moodiness had crept into his voice making Maggie regret her persistence. She'd never meant to cause him hurt; she just wanted to know more about him. And looking at him now, she realized too late the mistake she'd made.

Leaving his empty glass on the bar, he stood. Placing his hands on either side of hers, he leaned in close to her. "It's a hard way to live, Maggie. And if I can help it, I'm not going back there."

Even though he'd whispered the words, the sound of them seemed to reverberate throughout the room. The stubbornness in his voice had worked its way up to his eyes. The man who stood before her looked at her with a hardened gaze, his determination at leaving his past life behind evident.

He blinked and when she looked at him again, whatever she thought she'd seen reflected in his eyes was gone. The first to look away, Maggie picked up a damp cloth and concentrated on cleaning the top of the bar. At least some of her questions had been answered and knowing just a little bit about his past helped to understand the man he was now.

And just like the snap of fingers or the drop of a hat, he changed. Gone was the irritation and resentment, and in their place was the quick-witted man who'd come into town days ago.

"Enough of this conversation, Maggie. We've a dance hall to open." Throwing his arms wide, he turned around in a circle. "And I've yet to teach you the reel."

Amazed by how quickly he recovered, she had trouble keeping pace with him.

"Have all of the refreshments been ordered?"

"Yes. The kegs of root beer, and as you know, the sarsaparilla is here. The lemonade will be made fresh on Friday."

"What about the cucumber sandwiches and tea biscuits you ladies are so fond of?"

"I placed the order with the restaurant earlier this week."

"Good. I wish we lived closer to the sea so we could serve some sort of shellfish. I suppose we'll have to be happy with our country offerings."

Pulling off the apron she'd tied about her earlier, Maggie set it on a shelf. Coming around from behind the bar she said, "Maybe after we see how it goes this weekend we could look into serving a heartier menu."

"Like mutton?"

He was joking of course, but Maggie still felt alarm racing through her as visions of men with legs of lamb grasped in greasy hands came to mind—not at all what she wanted for her establishment.

"I hear it's a good farmer's meal."

Wondering why men had to be so exasperating, she said, "Mr. Clay, I'm sorry for bringing up your painful childhood memories."

"Ah, but that's where you're wrong. My childhood wasn't painful, it's just one I choose not to dwell on. What about your childhood, Maggie? What was yours like?"

Maggie looked at him. "I had a very nice childhood. My family comes from a small town downstate."

"Brothers, sisters?"

"I have one brother. I've always considered my cousins as my sisters. We gathered here at Aunt Margaret's for most of our summers. Unlike you seem to do, Mr. Clay, I hold my family very close to my heart." Wistfully she added, "They mean everything to me."

Her clear gaze studied him and as she saw his doubt at this, Maggie wondered why this concept seemed so hard for him to fathom. Then it dawned on her that perhaps Mr. Clay wasn't so fond of his family after all. Maybe he was even ashamed of where he came from. That thought horrified her.

Maggie's family, as frustrating as they could

be at times, meant the world to her. It was almost unthinkable to be ashamed of any one of them. No matter what any of them did, Maggie would still love them.

Obviously Mr. Clay felt differently about his family.

While she pondered those thoughts, Maggie walked around the hall fixing the tablecloths and moving the chairs into place. Slowly thoughts of Samuel Clay's family receded to the back of her mind.

Excitement over the grand opening had been building in town all week long. Everywhere were signs of the big event. Posters had been hung on every storefront window. Aunt Margaret had had Mr. Wagner place advertisements in newspapers as far away as New York City.

"Maggie, I need to go see about acquiring some extra rooms." Samuel interrupted her musings.

"I don't think there are any left at Mrs. Bartholomew's. She mentioned to me this morning that all of her rooms were already taken." Following him out the door, she called after him. "Mr. Clay, did you hear what I said?"

His answer was to give her a quick backwards wave over his shoulder. Men! she thought, always assuming they knew everything. He'd be back in a few minutes. Slowly it dawned on her.

Why did he need to see about reserving rooms? The trio of musicians, who would be arriving on the 3 o'clock train today, already had rooms.

As he hurried along the pebbled walkway, Sam heard Maggie call out to him. He knew the rooms were already reserved because he'd been the one doing the reserving. When the dance troupe arrived they would fill the boarding house. He just wanted to be sure everything was in order.

Whistling, Sam felt the excitement brewing inside of him. This dance troupe was one that had been performing for six months now. They were young, but were already showing great potential to one day be the best in the business and *he* had booked them for the grand opening. And that had been no easy feat.

Arriving in Albany, he'd learned that the group had already been hired at a local hall. Sam had almost been forced to buy out that contract in addition to paying them for performing in Surprise. However, he'd finessed his way around one very attractive female hotel manager and secured the group for himself without further ado or extra cost.

The delay had cost him extra time, but it would be well worth his effort just to see the look on

Maggie's face when the dancers appeared on her stage. He could almost picture the spark in those sky blue eyes of hers. The prim and proper Miss Monroe was going to learn how to kick up her heels.

If nothing else, it would certainly distract her from asking him any more personal questions. The woman had a bee stuck up in her bonnet where his life was concerned. When the fairer sex was involved, Sam made it a habit to never reveal too much. But with Maggie he acted differently. She had a way of getting him to say things that he otherwise wouldn't tell anyone.

He'd never spoken to another human being about his family before today. Perhaps it was the way she'd asked, or maybe it was because he'd needed to tell someone where he came from. Not that it mattered, because he was who he was. All the Maggies in the world, and especially one particular Maggie, couldn't change that—even if she wanted to try.

Chapter Ten

"Put the flowers over on the left side of the bar," Sam ordered the young man who was helping put the finishing touches on the decorations.

Flipping open his pocket watch for the tenth time, he checked the time. Fifteen minutes until the opening and from the low hum of voices outside the building, he'd guess everyone in the town was lined up out there in the streets.

"Mr. Clay!"

Turning at the frantic tone in her voice, he took one look at her and let out a low whistle. "Well, just look at you, Miss Maggie. All decked out like a birthday cake."

Wearing a low-cut, yellow, taffeta evening gown with short puffy sleeves, she looked stunning. Her blond locks were swept up into a bun with soft ringlets resembling spun gold framing her flushed face.

"Mr. Clay, where is the lemonade? I can't seem to find the batch I made earlier today anywhere."

Taking her by the shoulders he said, "Calm yourself, Maggie. The lemonade is already behind the bar with the other beverages."

"Yes, of course."

He felt her trembling beneath his touch. Behind them, two of the musicians were tuning up violins while another sat at the piano bench, fingers poised over the ivory keys.

"The platters of sandwiches and scones have also been put there. So you see there's no need to fret. We are ready," Sam added.

"I hope so. I've put a lot of effort and planning into the grand opening and I want everything to be perfect."

Her words wounded his pride. Quirking an eyebrow, he said, "You didn't do this by yourself."

"I'm sorry. I meant to say *we* put a lot of effort toward this evening."

"That's more like it."

"Did you see the crowd outside? I think everyone within a hundred miles has come to celebrate with us."

He watched, mesmerized as the pulse at the side of her throat moved up and down. Running a thumb lightly over the spot, he felt her excitement and the warmth of her smooth skin.

She turned her full attention to him, blue eyes searching his face in surprise. Without giving it another thought, Sam dipped his head and kissed her lightly on the lips. Her mouth was dewy soft beneath his.

Surprised when she didn't pull away, he was the first to detach himself from the kiss. Lifting his head, Sam watched her. The look in her eyes was mystifying, like she didn't know what to make of his actions.

Quickly, before she could say a word, he spoke. "That's for luck." Placing his arm about her waist, he turned so they were both facing the entryway. "Shall we greet our guests?"

"Yes," she simply replied.

Within minutes of opening the doors the hall was flooded with a mass of people. His attention, though, was focused on Maggie. Stepping away from his side, she greeted the guests as they came through the swinging louvered doors. A born hostess, he thought.

A light tap on his shoulder had him turning away from Maggie. He wasn't happy to see the stage manager who'd come with the dance troupe standing anxiously behind him.

Quickly, taking the man by the elbow, he ushered him through the growing throng of people to the back room. "What is the matter, Mr. Funk?"

"The girls are saying their dressing room is too small for the four of them. They want you to find them someplace else to get ready."

The balding man—who Sam knew for a fact wasn't more than twenty-five, but looked more like he was going to be passing nigh on his fortieth birthday—looked at him with a puffy red face.

"Look, Mr. Funk. They are going to have to make do with the space just for tonight. After the opening we can make other accommodations."

"I tried to tell them that, Mr. Clay. They want to hear it from you."

Quickly glancing over his shoulder, Sam checked to make sure that Maggie wouldn't miss him and escaped into the makeshift dressing room where the sounds of shrill, upset voices reached his ears.

Stepping aside like the man was afraid a plague was going to be tossed upon him, Mr. Funk let Sam enter the small space ahead of him.

Raising his hands in a peaceful gesture, Sam said, "Ladies, what's all the fuss about?"

"We can't even move around each other in here, Mr. Clay. This is not the agreement we made with you, sir." Rosy, the tallest woman in the troupe, said, her bosom heaving against the tight-fitting beaded fabric of her dance costume.

"Now ladies," he drawled in a placating tone. "I explained all of this before you came here. This is only a temporary dressing room, just for tonight."

"It isn't right for us, Mr. Clay," Susie, the smallest of the foursome, said in a squeaky voice. "You promised us a room with mirrors and dressing tables, one for each of us. Why, this is nothing more than a closet!"

Four beaded, brightly made-up women descended upon him. Raising his hands in a defensive gesture, he answered their complaint. "Ladies! Ladies! Before you send me out to be lynched, you need to be reasonable. You are, of course, right—this is nothing more than a closet."

The truth of it was that up until this morning this room had been a closet. One with wash buckets and mops piled into it. Sam was hoping that once Maggie saw the girls dance and the crowd's reaction to them, he could convince her to make the larger storage room behind the stage area into a permanent dressing room.

"Mr. Clay," Pearl, the blondest woman he'd ever laid eyes upon, said, "If you don't get this taken care of by tomorrow, we will be out of here."

"I will make certain that you have fresh flowers in your dressing room each night." Frantically he searched his mind for things that women love to be pampered with. "And in addition, there will be fresh drinking water and hot water for washing up with after the show."

While the four of them huddled together discussing this, Sam looked at Mr. Funk who was nervously shifting his weight from one foot to the other.

Pearl lifted her head and said, "We'd like a tub."

"And bath salts," Susie chirped.

Suppressing the urge to roll his eyes heavenward, Sam gave in to their demands, wondering how he was going to sneak a tub and a supply of bath salts by Maggie. He'd managed to get the girls into town without anyone being the wiser, so he supposed that the tub shouldn't be any more of a problem.

"Ladies, you have yourself a deal. I will see you out on the stage in one hour." Shaking his head, he left them to finish getting ready for the show.

The trio was ready to begin the first dance set, right after he and Maggie welcomed everyone.

Spotting her speaking to her aunt and cousins, Sam made his way to her. He stopped every few feet to greet people, so by the time he reached her he was out of breath.

Maggie watched him speaking and smiling to their patrons. He looked like a riverboat captain decked out in his black trousers and a black jacket. The rich, red brocade vest with its gold thread running throughout the fabric hugged a muscular chest covered by a crisp white shirt. It didn't escape her notice either that the man wearing it was very handsome indeed.

While Maggie had fretted for hours before getting dressed, she was quite certain the confident man had stepped into those clothes without a thought. Mr. Clay's ability to rise to any occasion never ceased to amaze her.

Repressing the urge to press her fingers against her lips, Maggie wondered about their kiss. He'd said it was for luck, but she'd felt much more. As calm as she may have appeared, Maggie had felt the heat from his lips pressed against hers clear down to her toes.

Trying not to put too much stock into the man's actions, she reminded herself that Mr. Clay, like most men, was an outrageous philanderer. The kiss was likely nothing other than a token of good luck, just as he'd said.

Why was it then, that his touch had left her yearning for something else?

As cool night air filtered in through the open windows, the orchestra began to play the first dance. Before Maggie knew what was happening, Mr. Clay swept her up in his arms, spinning her, in step with the waltz, out into the middle of the dance floor.

"Mr. Clay!" she gasped, trying to catch her breath. "I thought we had agreed to welcome our guests before the dancing was to begin."

Grinning at her in that wicked way of his, Mr. Clay replied, "I thought it would be much nicer to start the evening off with the first dance set, and for you to start calling me Sam."

"Sam." Using his given name made her feel like their relationship had taken yet another turn. While she was mulling this over, Sam continued talking as if nothing out of the ordinary had transpired.

"Then when our patrons—really, Maggie, you must stop thinking of them as our guests, they are, after all, paying customers. As I was saying, when our *patrons* take their first respite then we can take a few moments to welcome everyone."

Around and around the room they waltzed with their family and friends enjoying the festivities. Laughter and merriment abounded, all while Maggie was caught up in Samuel Clay's arms. Trying to remind herself that he was a rogue of the worst kind—the love-them-and-leave-them type, no doubt about it.

Still she fought with her sensibilities, trying to ignore how firm the muscles in his arms were and how the warmth from his hand pressed against her lower back penetrated the layers of clothing she wore, branding her skin. And worst of all, as other couples danced around them, she realized she enjoyed being part of a couple.

Maggie had to repeatedly remind herself that she didn't need a man to make her complete. She was a businesswoman in her own right and could very well stand on her own. But when he bent his head low, his warm breath grazing her ear, she felt the heat of a blush spreading across her cheeks. All of those thoughts flew from her mind like birds scattering from a tree.

"You're doing a great job, Maggie."

Smiling, she said, "I had a very good instructor. You still need to show me the steps to this reel you keep talking about."

"A simple two-step. You'll pick it up quickly.

Really, relax and enjoy the dance. After all the time and energy we put into getting this dance hall running it's time for us to have some fun!"

The waltz turned into a country reel and everyone formed two lines. Samuel stood across from her and when it was their turn they joined hands, sidestepping down the pathway formed by the two lines. She picked up the steps easily. Her heart racing, laughter bubbled up and burst from her like brilliant sunshine from a dried up rain cloud.

The first dance set ended, and still holding her hand firmly in his, Sam led her up the stairs onto the stage. Catching her breath, she said, "I think that was by far my favorite dance."

"You're a fast learner." Then he winked at her. "Go ahead, Miss Maggie, welcome your town to our establishment."

Letting go of his hand, she took center stage. Looking out over the crowd at all the happy, flushed people, Maggie felt contentment and a sense of accomplishment that she'd never felt before.

After taking a deep, fortifying breath, she spoke to her family and friends. "I'd like to thank you all for coming to our grand opening. It is my hope that this hall will come to represent yet another testament to the growth of the town of Surprise."

Cheers and clapping erupted as everyone got caught up in the moment. Catcalls and whistles soon followed. Flustered, Maggie looked around wondering what had caused the sudden change in the atmosphere.

Feeling Sam's hand against her back she turned to him in askance.

"Ah, ladies and gentlemen, as part of this evening's festivities, there are a few surprises."

Out of the corner of her eye, Maggie caught the sight of brilliant, colored dresses and long-legged women. As they galloped out onto the stage, she nearly passed out. They were barely dressed!

"Who are these women?" Fury turned whatever warmth she'd felt to ice. "What have you done, Samuel?"

Chapter Eleven

She watched in horror as four young women took to the stage, completely oblivious to the fact that Sam had pulled her off to one side. Leading her down the stairs, Maggie tripped and found herself catapulting into his arms.

"You . . . you!" Sputtering incoherently she tried to find the words that would express her outrage. She batted at his shoulders and chest.

Catching her by the wrist and righting her on the bottom step, he said, "Come on, Maggie. Try to enjoy the show."

The show turned out to be an American version of the popular French cancan. Dressed in matching pink ruffled skirts with frilly, overskirt bustles the girls twirled about the stage kicking their pink and blue striped stocking-covered legs over their heads.

Embarrassment flooded through her. She could barely bring herself to look at her family and friends. To make matters worse, the cheering from the audience drowned out any coherent thoughts.

"I will get you for doing this to me, Samuel," she ground out through clenched teeth. "You have ruined me."

Yanking her arm free from his hold, she stalked off to find her family. Aunt Margaret was sitting at a corner table with John Wagner. Flanking the couple were Lydia and Abigail.

Lydia sprung up from her seat and embracing Maggie, gushed in her usual exuberant way, "Maggie, you have quite a grand opening going on here! Why, I think everyone from the entire town is here."

Adding their good wishes, Abigail and Aunt Margaret both told her what a wonderful event this was. Above the din of the crowd, Aunt Margaret shouted, "The dancers were certainly a nice touch!"

A shudder ran through her when she thought of Samuel Clay's deceit. He was turning out to be nothing more than a lying, self-absorbed scoundrel. Looking at her cousins enjoying their evening out with their husbands, Maggie wondered at how easily they seemed to have found happiness.

She guessed it wasn't in the cards for her. Whatever attraction she thought she'd been feeling for Samuel was probably nothing more than a lapse in her otherwise good judgment.

Sam kept looking over the crowd hoping to catch Maggie's attention. He'd known exactly how she would react to the idea of the dance troupe, which was the sole reason he hadn't discussed it with her before tonight.

But the crowd was reacting with such fervor he knew the decision to bring the girls to Surprise had been a good one. Turning to face the stage, he watched as they performed the grand finale. All four girls threw back their heads, whooping loudly, and then with a good running start, they landed perfect splits at the edge of the stage.

Wild applause filled the hall. Rising from the floor the girls took their curtain call, bowing and curtsying their way off stage. After a few minutes the trio of musicians took their places.

Walking around the waltzing couples, Sam spotted Maggie behind the refreshment bar busily pouring lemonade into thick clear glasses. Seeing him, she turned her back to him.

"Mr. Clay, I've had a most enjoyable evening." This came from the mercantile owner, Mr. Jules. "This here dance hall is going to be a huge success. Miss Margaret certainly knows how to come up with good ideas."

He sipped the lemonade Maggie had slammed down in front of him a few minutes ago. "Putting you and Miss Maggie in charge was smart too." Lifting his glass, he toasted them.

Sam was all too aware of the cold, blue-eyed stare Maggie was casting his way. He shivered from it. Turning on the charm, he smiled his thanks to Mr. Jules while shaking the hands of Cole Stanton and Alexander Judson.

Slapping him on the back, Cole said, "Good job. The building came out real nice. Oh and Maggie, I like what you did with the paint." He winked at her and left to find his wife.

"The green is certainly a spirited color," Alexander laughed. "It's the first thing you see when you come into this end of town."

Sam caught the spray from the wet cloth used to wipe up spills from the bar as Maggie slapped it down on the wood slab in front of the men. The front of his new vest darkened with damp spots. Carelessly flicking his finger over one of the places where the water was soaking through, he hoped it wouldn't ruin the garment, which had cost him dearly.

Before he could let her know how he didn't appreciate the action, Maggie was stalking off. He lost sight of her halfway through the crowd.

"Looks to me like she's got a bee under her bonnet about something." John Wagner wiggled his bushy eyebrows at him. "Miss Margaret sent me over to tell you she'll be taking her leave now."

Following Mr. Wagner to where the matriarch waited near the doorway, Sam pasted a half-hearted smile on his face. Worrying over Maggie was going to be the death of him yet. And there she stood faithfully by her aunt's side, averting her gaze from his.

"Ah, Mr. Clay, there you are. What a wonderful evening I've had. Thank you so much. You and my niece have done a splendid job with this old building."

Bowing slightly, he said, "I'm glad you found our establishment up to your standards."

Taking hold of Maggie's hand, she replied, "I would expect nothing less from the two of you. Oh, and before I forget, we'll be having a meeting on Sunday after church to plan the upcoming box lunch social. And I expect you to attend, Maggie."

Dipping her head, she planted a kiss on her aunt's cheek. "I'll be there. Good night, Aunt Margaret. Mr. Wagner."

"I'll see you in the morning." Mr. Wagner wheeled the older woman out into the cool night.

Sam nodded at her. Right now he and Miss Maggie needed to finish out the evening.

"I'll see to tallying the revenue from the refreshments. You can say good night to our *guests.*"

Adjusting his cravat, he suppressed the urge to smile. Maggie was deliberately goading him by using the word *guests* instead of *patrons*, knowing full well how much the choice annoyed him.

"I think we should auction off the boxes and no bid should be lower than two cents." Lydia had a pencil poised over a tablet of paper. Sticking the end of the pencil in her mouth, she nibbled on it while concentrating on her notes.

Sitting on her aunt's verandah overlooking the town, Maggie was hardly contributing to the meeting. She still hadn't recovered from the grand opening of the dance hall. According to the receipts it had been a huge financial success, or so Mr. Clay had informed her.

Of course, she was learning she shouldn't put much stock in the words coming from his mouth.

She'd carefully avoided being alone with the wretched man since that night. It didn't matter at all how many compliments they'd received on the entertainment. And most of those came from the menfolk concerning the dance troupe. Maggie now thought of the four young women as "the vixens."

"This should help out the school a great deal," Lydia added.

"Maggie, you have barely said a word in the past hour. Is everything all right, dear?"

"Yes, Aunt Margaret. Fine and dandy," she quipped.

"Good. Then you won't mind making up a lunch for the picnic."

"What?" Maggie's thoughts weren't on the picnic.

"Food—cucumber sandwiches, peach pie, and the like." Lydia waved her hand in the air. "Honestly Maggie, whatever is wrong with you?"

"Man trouble," Abigail whispered.

"I am not having man trouble." Tears pricked the backs of her eyelids. Maggie left the wicker chair, walking to stand beside a porch post.

But her denial did not make Abigail's words any less true. For the first time in her life she was attracted to a man. And nothing was going the way she supposed it should. She'd done a fair job of avoiding Samuel for the past week, thinking that not seeing him would make her hurt feelings go away. But that hadn't been the case.

She kept remembering how he'd promised her they would share in every decision concerning the business. She'd trusted him and he'd thrown that trust right back in her face.

Stubborn pride was preventing her from speaking more than two civil words at a time to him. He'd apologized several times over and each time she shunned him. Now they worked together in uneasy silence.

Confusion left her feeling as if her carefully planned life was out of control like a wild unbroken horse. Standing here on Aunt Margaret's porch Maggie knew she was going to have to fix what was wrong and soon, otherwise she was going to make herself crazy.

Chapter Twelve

Women in bright gingham dresses and men in their Sunday best milled around the yard behind the schoolhouse. The sun riding high in the cloudless sky dried the dew soaked grass, making for perfect picnic conditions.

Samuel Clay tipped his hat to every lady and shook a few of the gentlemen's hands, though all the while his gaze searched the gathering for Maggie. The stubborn woman hadn't spoken to him since the grand opening. At first it had been a game, and he assumed once the dust settled, so to speak, she would forgive him.

This had yet to happen.

With the noon hour approaching, everyone

began to gather at the foot of the steps leading to the schoolhouse entrance. Here a podium had been set up. Red, white, and blue bunting looped through the white handrails fluttering in the breeze. Baskets and boxes of all shapes and sizes filled the steps.

"Mine is the one with the bright pink ribbon tied onto the handle," a woman behind him whispered to the man standing next to her.

Wondering how and if Maggie had decorated her basket, he paid closer attention to the lunches. By his estimation there were close to fifty of them and after several frustrated minutes of searching, he couldn't decide which one might be hers.

"If I were you, I'd bid on the one with the yellow cloth lining."

Sam turned to find Abigail's husband nodding to him.

Nudging his arm, Cole added, "Second step, third one on the right side."

"Thanks, I owe you one."

Now that he knew what Maggie's lunch looked like, he walked over to the big shade tree and leaned against it, waiting for his turn to bid.

John Wagner came out of the school and stepped up to the podium. Picking up the auctioneer's gavel, he whacked it twice calling everyone to attention.

"I'd like to welcome all of you fine citizens to the first annual box lunch social. The proceeds from today's event will go toward the purchase of school supplies for our children. So dig deep and bid high!"

The bidding began and much to his dismay, Mr. Wagner started with the lunches closest to him. This meant Maggie's basket wouldn't come up to the auction block until near the end. Preparing for the wait, Sam loosened his neatly tied cravat and unbuttoned his shirt cuffs, rolling the sleeves up to his elbows.

Soon the yard and hillside were full of picnic goers enjoying their crisply cooked chicken, hard-boiled eggs, and in some cases, full three course meals. The sheriff and her husband took a spot behind the tree where Sam was waiting. Within minutes Lydia and Alexander joined them with their two children in tow.

As the crowd thinned out, Sam began to wonder about the contents in Maggie's basket. He didn't even know if she could cook. He'd never seen her cook. For all he knew she might not even have the talent to do something as simple as butter a slice of bread.

He saw her going up the stairs with her basket in hand. Unlike the other women who had dressed in their Sunday best, Maggie wore a black skirt and a long-sleeved, high-collared, white blouse. He smiled, shaking his head. Maggie wasn't going to give an inch. It was almost as if she'd known he was going to be the sole bidder and had dressed for the occasion.

So be it. Sam was up to the challenge.

Lifting the yellow cloth, John Wagner peered into the basket. "Ah, what have we here? I see a jar of pickled beets."

Not one of Sam's favorite foods.

"Two sandwiches—smells like ham to me—and for dessert there are two big slices of apple pie."

At least the ham and pie were to his liking.

"Let's start the bidding at ten cents. Do I hear ten cents for Miss Maggie's basket?"

An older gentleman whom Sam didn't recognize raised his hand. Catching Mr. Wagner's eye, Sam nodded.

"I see we have ten cents and I believe Mr. Clay here would like to raise the bid?"

Sam nodded again and held up two fingers.

"Twenty cents. We have twenty cents, do I hear twenty-five?"

The man raised up five fingers indicating a fifty cent bid. Sam didn't know who this fellow was, but there was no way he was going to outbid him. So raising his hand, he too held up five fingers.

"Mr. Clay, we already have a bid of fifty cents."

"My bid is for five dollars."

A hush fell over the crowd. He didn't dare look at Maggie's face, but he heard her yelp.

"Mr. Clay, are you certain you want to bid five dollars for this lunch? It is, after all, only two sandwiches, pie, and the pickled beets."

"Well, you can toss out the beets. I don't care much for them anyway." Pushing away from the tree he made his way over to the podium to collect his winnings. Stepping out from the shade into the bright sunlight, he caught his first glimpse of his lunch companion's face.

Looking madder than a wet hen, she sailed down the steps. Sam passed her halfway up. After paying Mr. Wagner the five dollars, he went to find her. Standing off by the corner of the building, she waited with the basket in hand and a folded patchwork quilt lying over one arm.

"Howdy, ma'am. Where would you like to sit?"

Turning a cold back to him, she walked away,

leaving him with no choice except to follow in her wake. *So much for lighthearted conversation,* he thought.

She was spreading the quilt on the ground under a small tree. Dappled sunlight covered them. While she pulled things out of the basket, tossing them carelessly on the quilt, he stood in stunned silence observing her quiet temper tantrum.

"You sure can carry a grudge, Maggie."

Without batting an eyelash, she commanded, "Sit down."

"Not yet. We need to settle this argument once and for all. Look, Maggie, I told you I was sorry for bringing those girls here without telling you first."

"No, you look, Mr. Clay. I didn't slave away in the kitchen for half the morning so this food could go to waste." Tossing the empty basket behind her, she busied herself by adjusting the ribbon holding back her blond locks.

"You took that much time preparing lunch for me?"

"Now how was I supposed to know *you* would be the one buying my basket?"

"Lucky guess?" he winked at her.

He thought he saw her thawing just a little bit.

"Sit before you cause even more of a scene

than you already have by bidding such a ridiculously high amount of money on what is probably the worst lunch here."

Kneeling next to her, he picked up one of the sandwiches and pulled off the wrapper. Taking a big healthy bite, he savored the rich flavor of the slow cooked ham. "Mmm. This is good."

"Of course it's good."

"I hadn't added cooking to your list of skills."

"Is that a compliment, Mr. Clay?"

"Let's just say you certainly know how to satisfy a man's appetite." He'd leaned in close to her to whisper the words and was quite satisfied with the warm blush making its way along her neckline.

He was definitely making headway.

Pushing him away, Maggie bit into her sandwich. After chewing thoughtfully for a few minutes, she swallowed. Dabbing daintily at the corners of her mouth with a napkin, she said, "If you wish to make changes in the entertainment for our dance hall, I'd like you to consult me beforehand."

Those were the first civil words she'd spoken to him in almost two weeks and Sam knew she was extending an olive branch to him. Not one to be foolish, he said, "I can do that."

"I'd like to know why you didn't do it to

begin with. You could have avoided all of this if you had."

"I knew you'd never approve of my plan."

"I wouldn't have."

"So how is this going to change our arrangement?"

Sighing, she looked at him. "I'll have to learn to compromise."

Laughing, he said, "You don't need to make it sound like a death sentence."

"In case you have failed to notice, Samuel, I don't like to compromise. I'm stubborn and set in my ways."

"You're also warm-hearted and very pretty." He spoke softly, the words for her ears only.

She fixed a clear blue-eyed gaze on him, leaving Sam mesmerized.

"You didn't have to say that. I know that I'm not the most sought after woman in this town."

His fingers touched hers. "I'm only telling you what I see. And right now I see a warm, intelligent, headstrong woman. One that I'm very glad to have as my business partner."

"You know statements like that could get you thrown out of every saloon in a hundred mile radius."

"I'm a progressive thinker."

"You're confident, steadfast, and for the most part true to your word."

"So what do you think about having the dance troupe here once each month?"

"Do we have to decide on this today?"

Knowing that their truce was tenuous, he conceded. "We can talk about it another time, but if the answer is yes, then I can get them booked before their schedule fills up."

"Sam, I'm not sure the girls are right for us."

Leaning back on his elbows, Sam looked out over the hillside. Blades of green grass bent to the wind and children ran around their parents laughing and playing. Miss Margaret was situated in the center of all the activity, ever the matriarch of the town.

Maggie had to agree to his idea. He needed the money. There was no way he was going to return to the farm now. He would never turn his back on his family, but he wasn't a farmer. Sam was an entrepreneur and if not for sharing this venture with Maggie, he might never have realized his dreams.

"Maggie, do you know how much money we made the other night?"

"I think it was near two hundred dollars."

Shaking his head, he replied, "It was more like

three hundred! Those girls made people want to stay and have fun. If patrons are having fun then they are spending money."

From the opposite end of town came the shrill sound of the train whistle as it pulled to a stop. More people coming to see if everything being said by the papers about the town was true, he supposed.

"The whole point of this business was to provide a place for people to be able to go and forget about their troubles."

"I understand this, Samuel, truly I do. It's just that you and I don't have the same idea about what will make us successful."

He could see she was getting angrier. He let out a frustrated sigh. "Oh shoot, Maggie. Did you have any fun at all the other night?"

He sensed her reluctance in answering. "Did you have fun, Maggie?" Rubbing his thumb on the tender underside of her wrist, he coaxed her response.

"Yes I did."

"Tell me when you were the happiest."

"When I was dancing with you."

That wasn't the answer he expected to hear and he knew what it took for her to admit she'd enjoyed being in his arms.

Quietly, he replied, "I'm glad I can make you feel happy." And he meant it.

Gazing at him intently, Maggie frowned. "I've never met anyone like you, Samuel. One minute you have me feeling frustrated and angry while the next you make me laugh."

He didn't know what to say. When he'd come to this town the last thing on his mind had been falling for a woman. And yet, here he was sitting next to this pretty young lady feeling the best he'd felt in months.

Tugging her up from the blanket, he gathered her in his arms. "Dance with me, Maggie."

"Here?"

Ignoring her protest, Sam began waltzing with her around the edges of the blanket.

"Samuel! Stop it this instant. People are staring at us." Playfully she swatted his arm.

"I want you to have fun with me, Maggie. Say the words, tell me you're having fun."

A few more spins around the blanket had them both laughing. "I am having fun!" Slowly they came to a stop and Sam couldn't resist dropping a kiss on the tip of her nose.

He heard her quick intake of breath and saw the brilliance of her gaze. "Sam, I . . . think we . . ."

He cut off her words with a kiss on those perfect lips, murmuring, "Don't think so much, Maggie."

She stood on her tiptoes, tentatively returning his kiss. Pulling away from her was hard for him to do because he liked the feel of Maggie Monroe's soft lips on his. He enjoyed the taste of salt on her mouth. But considering they were standing in a very public place with many townsfolk as witnesses he decided it was for the best.

Settling back on the blanket, they spent the next hour watching three-legged and sack races. They laughed at the antics of the youngsters, and howled at the clumsiness of the older folks. Offering Maggie his hand, he helped her up from the quilt. Together they packed the basket and folded the blanket.

"Mr. Clay!" He turned at the sound of Mrs. Bartholomew's voice. "Mr. Clay, there's some people here to see you."

Handing the blanket to Maggie, Sam looked around.

"He's right over there by Maggie." Mrs. Sutherland was leading an older couple and a young man to him.

"Samuel! Samuel! I can't believe we've finally found you. At last!"

Speechless, he could only stare open-mouthed at the people approaching him.

Chapter Thirteen

Springing to her feet, Maggie brushed the dust from her skirt, noticing right away that Samuel hadn't moved forward to greet the newcomers. There was a look on his face she'd never seen before.

Touching his arm, she said, "Samuel, do you know these people?" She felt the muscles in his upper arms tense beneath her touch.

She didn't understand his reaction. The woman and gentleman didn't look like they meant any harm. And the young man walking beside them looked as if he wouldn't hurt a fly.

"Samuel," she whispered.

Hands stuffed into his pockets, he went to join

the people. Sensing his reluctance to do so, Maggie followed a few steps behind, curiosity getting the best of her.

When he didn't turn to introduce them, she made a movement as if to step into their circle. Sam held up his arm, stopping her. There were tears in the woman's eyes as she looked up at him. The man with his hand at her waist was equally emotional.

"Maggie, these people are my family."

"My goodness! It's my pleasure to finally meet you."

Now she could see the similarities. The woman's eyes were the same color as Samuel's and the hair on the younger man was of a similar shade.

"How did you find me?"

The sound of his voice interrupted her musings. He wasn't happy to see them. Why? She wondered.

"We saw a picture of you in this here paper. Show him the one, Walter."

The young man, who Maggie realized couldn't be more than halfway through his teen years, took a dog-eared, wrinkled newspaper out of his coat pocket. Handing it to Samuel, he smiled shyly.

Sam snapped the paper open with such force the page tore. She recognized the picture of them. It had been taken the day of the grand opening. She and Samuel were standing in front of the dance hall. Maggie hadn't imagined the picture would be publicized so much. The reporter from the *Albany Times* obviously thought the photograph would make his review of the opening better.

Maggie didn't like the way she looked in the picture. Her hair was pulled back in a tight bun and on that particular day she'd been cleaning. So she'd been wearing an old brown dress that made her look old and prudish. Samuel was wearing his typical garb and looked as handsome as ever.

Taking matters into her own hands she stepped forward. "I'm Maggie Monroe. Welcome to Surprise."

Sam's father stepped forward. Extending his hand to her, he said, "I'm Daniel Clay and this is my wife, Emma, and our youngest son Walter."

Feeling a bit stupefied she took his hand in hers and shook it. It took all of her control not to knock Samuel off his feet. His treatment of his family was deplorable to say the very least and she wasn't going to stand for it.

Looking from him to his father, she quipped, "I can certainly see the family resemblance."

Candidly she added, "You'll have to forgive your son. I'm afraid that living here in this small town must have addled his brain a bit more than I first thought."

Sam's hand gripped her shoulder. "I don't need you to be making excuses for me, Maggie."

"Might I suggest that you welcome your family to our little town properly?"

Carrying the same stiffness in his posture that she'd noticed earlier, he moved toward them. "Mother, Father. It's good to see you. You're both looking well. And Walter, I don't believe I would have recognized you; you've grown so much."

The insincerity in his tone had her chomping down on her lower lip in frustration. And he thought *she* was stubborn?

"How long will you be staying in town?" Maggie asked Mrs. Clay.

"We're not sure. We've already done some inquiring and it seems there aren't many extra rooms left in your boarding houses."

"I'm sure we can find a place for you to stay while you're here. Perhaps Samuel will be so kind as to give up his room for you."

Beside her she thought she heard him choking. Daring to look at him, she saw the color of his face was a most brilliant shade of red. Giving him a good strong whack between his shoulder blades, she offered, "There, that should be better."

He glared at her. "Might I have a word with you?" Without waiting for her answer he grabbed hold of her elbow, propelling her across the grassy knoll out of hearing distance of his family.

"What do you think you're doing?"

"I'm trying to be nice to your family. Samuel, whatever has gotten into you? Your family has obviously gone to great lengths to find you. The least you can do is act like you're happy to see them."

"I am."

Folding her arms across her chest, she studied his face. She wondered why he was looking so forlorn and troubled. "Samuel? Tell me what's going on."

Spreading out his arms, he gave her one of his false smiles. "The time isn't right for them to be here. That's all there is to it."

A warm breeze filtered through the glade, rising up over the land where they were standing. Turning her face toward the sky, Maggie let the air caress her skin. It reminded her of the way Samuel's touch felt, feather light and soft. Taking a calming breath, she turned to find him walking away from her.

She'd never seen him like this. Even when

she'd painted the outside trim that awful green, he hadn't been this upset.

With a quick glance over her shoulder, she saw his family still standing there alone on the hill-side. Picking up her skirts, she ran after him.

Catching up to him, she latched on to his arm. Pulling him around to face her, she implored, "They came all this way to see you, Samuel. The very least you can do is take them someplace where they will be comfortable and you can talk."

"I don't want to do that, Maggie. And I don't want you interfering in this."

Tears stung her eyes. In the space of a few short minutes the happiness she'd felt evaporat-ed. Looking into his hazel eyes, she saw a stranger. How could she have believed there could be something more than friendship between them?

Dropping her arms to her side, she replied as calmly as she could, "Very well then. I won't bother you over this matter any further." Stepping away from him, she went back to the small family.

"Maggie! Wait!"

Rushing along she hurried to put as much space between them as possible. "Leave me alone, Samuel." Waving him off, she joined the

Clays. The very least she could do was make them feel welcome.

"Why don't you let me see about finding you some rooms?"

"That would be lovely, Miss Monroe. But I'm sure our eldest will help us out."

Looking back toward the knoll, Maggie didn't see any sign of Samuel. "I'm going to speak to my aunt. You wait right here until I come back."

Tramping down the hill she found her aunt sitting under the big oak tree talking with Lydia and Abigail. Quickly interrupting them, she explained the predicament of the Clays being in town with no place to stay. And just as she'd hoped, Aunt Margaret felt called to action.

Making her way back up the hill she found the Clays right where she'd left them. "Mr. and Mrs. Clay, Walter. My aunt has graciously offered the use of several rooms in the guest wing of her home."

"Oh my, this is too much to ask of a complete stranger. It would be such an imposition."

"Nonsense. My aunt has enough room in her house to take in half the town." Smiling, she held out her hand to the older woman.

When she took it in hers, Maggie felt the time-worn calluses of someone who'd worked a great deal. Remembering that Samuel had told her of the family farm, she asked, "How did you manage to get time away from your farm?"

A look of anguish crossed between the couple. "If you don't mind Miss, it's a matter we wish to discuss with our son first."

Nodding, Maggie wondered when that might be. For people who had most certainly been traveling for hours and had to be weary down to their bones, they had the patience of saints where their son was concerned.

Maggie thought his ears deserved a good boxing. "All right then. Let's get you settled. Did you leave your bags at the station?"

"The clerk at the telegraph office said we could leave them with him until we found a room."

Aunt Margaret and Mr. Wagner found them just as they reached the path leading to the house. "There you are, Maggie. Please, introduce me to my guests."

"Aunt Margaret, this is Emma and Daniel Clay and their youngest son, Walter."

"It's a pleasure to meet you. I'm so glad you'll be staying with us. My housekeeper, Anna, can help you get your things up to the guest rooms."

Aunt Margaret prudently left out the fact that they were Samuel's long lost family.

"Did I hear you say your bags are at the telegraph office?"

"Yes," Mr. Clay answered.

"John, why don't you and Mr. Clay and—Walter, is it?—take care of retrieving their belongings while we ladies get settled."

"Come along with me, gentlemen. I think the ladies wish to be alone."

As the men ambled off, Maggie helped her aunt up the flower-lined walkway. She'd been so busy, she'd hardly noticed that Aunt Margaret had graduated from the wheelchair to using a cane to aid her in getting around.

Anna greeted them at the door, holding it open for them. "Come in. I see we have company."

"Anna, this is Samuel Clay's mother, Emma. His father and brother went back to town with Mr. Wagner to get their luggage. They will be staying with us indefinitely."

"Oh, no. We will not be imposing for that long. I'm sure a room will become available soon." Emma spoke in soft dulcet tones.

Maggie wondered how this petite woman could be Samuel's mother. "It is no imposition. We love to have guests and it's been a long time since any have stayed here."

The foyer felt cool after being out in the noon-day sun, though the coolness did little to chill her hot anger.

Chapter Fourteen

Taking a stance in the doorway to the lumberyard office, Samuel watched his mother being escorted to the house on the hill. He didn't know how to tell Maggie that he hadn't run from them because he didn't want them around. He'd done so because he was scared.

"Looks to me like our friend here has some troubles," Cole said, nudging Alexander in the side with his elbow.

"Trouble just seems to follow me around," he scoffed.

Putting his arm around Samuel's shoulder, Alexander said, "Tell you what, why don't we go into my office, out of sight of the women, and have some libations?"

"Sounds good to me," he replied.

Cole led the way to the back office. Opening the bottom desk drawer he pulled out a bottle and three tumblers. When Samuel looked at him questioningly, Cole said, "Sometimes a man's got to have a little sustenance to get through the rough spots."

Sitting in the straight-backed chair facing the desk, he accepted the glass Cole handed him. Alexander took a seat behind the desk, while Cole leaned back against the wall. Silently they sipped.

Alexander was the first to speak. "So those people, they're your kinfolk?"

Nodding, Sam tossed back another swallow of the whiskey.

"You know most people in these parts would be pleased to see their family. I couldn't help but notice that you seem anything but."

"I wasn't expecting to see them for several more months. They caught me off guard is all."

"They look like decent people to me," Cole said.

"They are." And this was a big part of what was bothering him. His father, mother, and brother were decent, plain people who worked hard to earn a living. What possessed them to leave the farm and go out into the world searching for him?

"Looks to me like Miss Maggie and her aunt took a liking to them from the start," Alexander noted.

Sam frowned at him, once again knowing that he should be happy that Maggie and his family had appeared to have taken a liking to one another so quickly.

Cole said, "You've got to hand it to the Monroe women, they sure know how to make a body feel welcome."

"Most of the time Maggie gives me nothing but grief." Slumping in the chair, he gulped down the rest of the whiskey, thinking about the times when she wasn't giving him grief. The times when she smiled at him, or laughed with him, those were the times when just being in the same room with her warmed his soul.

Cole and Alexander exchanged knowing glances. "That's the way it is with those women, from the beginning, anyway," Cole commented.

"Then they get under your skin and worm their way into your heart and before you know it, you're married to one of them." Alexander added with a knowing smile.

Folding his arms across his chest, Sam stared

at the two of them in disbelief, declaring, "I'm not ready to marry Maggie Monroe."

"So you say right now." Cole laughed.

"Look, I've got bigger problems right now."

He stood and set the empty glass on the desk. Nodding to both men, he left. Standing in the middle of the road, he looked around, unable to decide what to do next. He supposed he could just confront his father and get all of the questions out of the way, or he could go to work at the dance hall. Better yet, he could just go to his room and sulk.

About to walk off in that direction, he caught sight of his father, brother, and John Wagner making their way down the walkway with three large traveling bags and one trunk between them.

Knowing he couldn't very well ignore them, he stepped between them, taking one of the bags from his father's timeworn hand. Thankfully there was no need for conversation on his part for Mr. Wagner chattered nonstop like a magpie the whole way to Margaret's home.

Samuel wondered at the man's capacity for useless banter.

The door to the house was already open when they arrived. With little fanfare the men set the bags down in the center of the hall. Sam was once again struck by the magnificence of the house. The claret-colored carpeting was lush under their feet.

Vases of flowers were placed neatly on side tables and the entire home smelled of lemony furniture polish. He realized with a start that Maggie had come out into the hallway. Silhouetted in the afternoon shadows, she watched him.

He found it curious how calm she appeared to be. Wispy tendrils of blond hair framed her face and those clear blue eyes were void of the anger he'd witnessed earlier. He couldn't help wondering if perhaps this was the calm before the storm.

Any minute she would pounce on him trading barbs, making him confess his thoughts and deep dark secrets. She had a way of making him say things he wouldn't otherwise share. He almost smiled at the thought. It seemed Cole and Alexander were right—she was getting under his skin. He wasn't so sure she'd fully wormed her way into his heart yet, though.

"Gentlemen, I see you found the luggage. Anna will show you to your rooms."

The tall housekeeper seemed to materialize out of thin air, ready to do her job.

"She's already put fresh water and towels there for you to wash up with. I'm sure after such a long trip you'd like to get rid of the road dust."

"Thank you, Miss Monroe. That's right kind of you." Samuel's father practically fell over himself shaking Maggie's hand while Walter stood shyly off to one side. A schoolboy blush spread across his face.

"Aunt Margaret and I will be awaiting your return in here." Gesturing behind her, Maggie showed them the sitting room.

With his father and brother following the housekeeper upstairs, Sam was left in the hallway with Maggie. Uncertain as to what to do next he looked to her with a sideways glance.

"Samuel, might I have a word with you outside?" Without waiting for his reply she walked ahead of him out the front door.

He'd no choice but to follow.

"Your mother is exhausted from their trip. Try to be nice to her."

"Of course I'll be nice to her."

Turning, she looked at him fiercely. "Would you mind telling me why their coming here has you so upset? It's quite obvious they love you very much. And dare I say, though Lord knows why, they seem to have missed you."

Shoving his hands in his pockets in frustration, he looked down the hill at the town. "They aren't here because they missed me. Something is wrong."

Distress etched her features. "You think someone is sick?"

"Good grief, Maggie. Don't be such an alarmist. I'm not sure what's going on."

"There's only one way to find out. Ask them."

He wished he had her fortitude. Maggie never skirted around any issue; her forthrightness was one of the things he admired about her. If she wanted to know something, she'd come right out and ask. Tenacity—that's what she had, and it's what he needed right now.

"As soon as they've rested up from the trip I'll speak with them."

"Good. They should be ready in half an hour."

"You don't give an inch do you, Maggie?"

"Not where family is concerned I don't."

He saw the sincerity reflected in her eyes and the stubborn set of her very attractive jaw line. It made him wonder when he'd become so cynical.

"I can't go back to their way of life."

"No one is asking you to."

"You don't know that. The reason they're here could very well be to drag me back to save the farm." Raking his hands through his hair, he declared, "I won't do it, Maggie!"

She must have sensed his anguish. Placing her hand on his shoulder, she said, "You don't even know what brought them here. Wait until you find out and then you can decide what needs to be done."

He conceded. "All right."

She left him standing with his back to her. She paused before going inside, saying softly, "And whatever is wrong, you don't have to do this alone."

Turning, he was going to thank her, but she was already inside the house. Taking a deep breath for fortitude, he walked through the entryway. Following the sound of female voices he was about to enter the sitting room when his father's voice stopped him.

"Samuel."

He thought his father looked tired. With a face wrinkled from the hours spent out of doors working, the tall figure from his memories was now slightly hunched over at the shoulders. His hair had thinned somewhat giving him a slightly older appearance than when Sam had last seen him.

"Would it be all right with you if we talked outside on the porch?"

To call it a porch was putting it mildly. What surrounded three quarters of Miss Margaret's home was a wide, pillared verandah. He didn't correct his father. To this man anything that stuck out from the front of a house was a porch.

Gesturing for his father to sit in one of the

white wicker chairs, Sam joined him. An awkward silence stretched between them.

His father broke the silence, saying, "Those are some fancy duds you're wearing, son. They suit you."

"Thanks."

Settling into the plump seat cushions, his father set the chair to rocking. "How are things with you?"

"Fine. As you know I was fortunate enough to get a job managing a dance hall." Resting his elbows on his knees, Samuel said, "I still have time left on our agreement, Pa."

A frown furrowed his father's brow. "You think that's why we're here, son? To take you back to the farm?"

"Well, aren't you?"

"We sold the farm."

Sam's head snapped up. "Why?"

"I'm not as young as I used to be, Samuel. Walter's been a help, but the land got to be more than we could handle. And there was no telling if you were coming back."

Guilt mingled with more than a little regret at the news. "I'm sorry to hear that," he said and he meant it. While farming hadn't been in his blood, it was his father's life, just as it had been for two generations before him.

He knew what it must have cost his father to give up the land and the legacy.

"We got a real good offer from a gentleman out of New York City. He wants to build a big house on the property." He sat there with his hands dangling at the side of the chair. "It's more money than I'd seen in my lifetime." He smiled at bit at the thought.

"If it's what you wanted to do then I'm pleased for you. But why did you come here?" The question was out of his mouth before he could stop from asking.

His father turned to give him a hard look. "We came to see our son. It's been going on how many years now, Sam, two and a half, nearly three? I wanted you to know that our deal is complete."

"I'm sorry. I didn't mean my words to sound like I'm not happy to see my family. I am. I've missed you too."

Rising from the chair, he looked out over the town. "And I'm glad our deal is done."

"So now you can get on with your life."

Isn't that what he wanted all along, to have his own life? He should feel relieved that he could move on, free from the guilt of leaving his family behind. And yet, a part of him wished it could have turned out differently for his father.

"I've got to get back to work."

"It was nice having this chat with you, Samuel."

"You too." He left his father relaxing on the verandah.

Chapter Fifteen

Letting the curtain fall from her hand, Maggie turned to face Mrs. Clay. She assumed when Samuel left the verandah that he was still upset with his father. Maggie would have liked nothing more than to follow him, giving him a piece of her mind. When she made a movement to leave, however, Mrs. Clay stopped her.

"Maggie, sometimes it's best to let a man stew in his own juices for a while." Patting the spot next to her on the sofa, she bade, "Come and tell me about this dance hall you and my son are running."

Her voice was so soft and quiet that Maggie

couldn't imagine her ever raising it in anger or otherwise. It was too bad Samuel hadn't inherited this trait. Sitting next to the woman, Maggie studied her.

"Samuel looks so different." With a wistful glance, Mrs. Clay continued to engage her in conversation.

"I don't know what he looked like before I met him, so I'm afraid I've nothing to compare him to." Maggie could well imagine him, though, in little cotton overalls with dirt smudges on the knees.

Taking a handkerchief from her silk purse, his mother dabbed at the corners of her eyes. Feeling sorry for the woman, Maggie placed a comforting hand over hers.

"He was always so restless—wanting more out of life, never content with his lot. I'm afraid my eldest did not like growing up on a farm." Smiling ruefully, she added, "Of course he'd no choice in the matter, not when he was just a boy. But as he grew to manhood, it was clear to me he would leave us."

"I'm sorry he did that."

"Please don't be. He wouldn't have been happy on the farm. The way he dresses now, I hardly recognize the man he's become."

Grinning at her observation, Maggie replied, "He is a bit flashy with his attire. I told him he looks like a riverboat captain."

Thoughtful for a moment, Mrs. Clay looked at Maggie. "He's so handsome. Is he happy here?"

Taken aback by the question and more so by the fact that she thought Maggie would know the answer to the question, she fussed with the tea service on the sofa table, gathering her thoughts.

"Yes, I suppose he's happy." Maggie knew his being here made her happier. She realized with a start that her world seemed brighter when he was around. "He certainly has quite the knack for running the hall."

"As soon as we're settled I'd love to go see the place. It's not too difficult to imagine Samuel running such an establishment."

"He enjoys his job, Mrs. Clay." She meant what she said. Samuel may be outspoken and a complete buffoon where Maggie was concerned, but he did like what he was doing with his life now.

Shifting on the sofa, she found Maggie's hand and said, "I think he enjoys his job because of you."

Flustered by her comment, Maggie quickly rose and made a great show of stacking the dirty teacups and saucers on the silver serving tray. She wasn't so sure about that. With the way

Samuel was goading her one minute and then flirting with her the next, it was hard to tell sometimes if he liked her or not.

From behind her Mrs. Clay said, "Trust me. A mother knows these things about her son. If you'll excuse me, I think I'll go join my husband on the porch."

Picking up the tray, Maggie made her way back to the kitchen thinking that she and Samuel had a lot to discuss.

Three days had passed since his family had arrived. Three days of self-imposed asylum. In that time he quickly adopted Maggie's habit of slamming things around. Of course, slamming glasses on the counter did little to alleviate his frustration. And if the number of broken glasses was any indication, he would be better off finding another way to vent his frustration.

Sam was in the middle of sweeping up the shards of glass when Maggie walked into the hall. Dust motes rode in on beams of sunshine as she threw open the window shutters. Then, pushing back the curtains, she raised the sashes, letting in a dusty breeze.

"You might be better off leaving those closed. Can't you see I'm trying to sweep up the dust?" he grumbled at her.

Turning, she faced him with her hands on her hips. "I see your mood hasn't improved since I last saw you."

He snorted. "I don't have much to be happy about."

Sighing loudly, she started taking the chairs down from the table tops where they'd been placed after closing last night. When they were all down and set around the tables, she went to the stack of freshly laundered linens and set about snapping a square of fabric over each table.

The tension stretched, straining the air around them until Sam thought he might suffocate from wanting it to break. He wasn't as good as she was at playing this game. She knew that.

Finally, he said, "I've done something I'm not very proud of, Maggie."

"I assume you're speaking of your family?"

Nodding, he stood the broom against the back wall behind the counter. "I suppose I should have told you this sooner."

"Go on." Without breaking her stride, she continued to set up the room.

"As you know, I didn't like farming. But what you don't know is that before I left, my father and I made a deal. If I could prove to him that I could make it on my own in three years, then I wouldn't have to return to the farm."

"I see."

Coming around in front of her, he took the napkins from her and held on to her hands. They trembled in his. "I don't think you do. Please, I'm begging you, don't let this change what's between us."

He saw the tears forming in her eyes and felt horrible.

"I have feelings for you, Samuel. Deep feelings and I'm trying very hard not to let this color my opinion of you. But I must ask—how could you have put your father in such a position? Forcing him to let you go, perhaps even forcing him to sell the land which he loved."

"It wasn't like that. We came to an amicable agreement. He understood why I was leaving."

Resting her hand alongside his cheek, Maggie looked into his eyes. "I'm so sorry for you. You spoke to your father about this?"

"We did at Miss Margaret's. He told me he was all right with the decision. The man from New York City gave them a great deal of money. More than any of us has ever seen. This matter isn't about us. My life is here and I wouldn't barter it away for any reason."

Leaning in toward him, she kissed him lightly on the mouth. "Somehow, I can't picture you as a farmer. Didn't you miss them at all when you left?" She wanted to understand Samuel.

"I missed them, but not their way of life."

"Your mother knew you were leaving."

He'd missed her the most. She was the one who'd understood how he'd felt about the land from the very beginning. Still, she hadn't sided with either him or his father. Instead she had just let them sort it out on their own.

"Samuel, make your peace with this." Maggie was standing in front of him now, balancing a pile of bright yellow napkins in her arms.

"I will. Maggie, do you think there is a future for the two of us?"

Her reply froze on her lips when Lydia came running into the hall.

"Come quickly! It's Abigail!"

Chapter Sixteen

"What's wrong with her?" Maggie asked.

"She's fainted." Lydia raced on down the street with Maggie and Samuel following close at her heels. "We were talking in her office when suddenly she just keeled over. Her face hit the desktop landing smack on a pile of wanted posters."

By the time they reached the sheriff's office, Cole and Alexander were assisting Abigail to one of the jail cell bunks. Maggie could see the ghostly whiteness of her face and feared there was something seriously wrong with her cousin.

"Oh my," she breathed, "she looks terrible."

"Has she eaten anything today?" Sam asked the obvious question.

"She's been having trouble keeping food down for the past week."

Silence greeted Cole's answer.

Lydia looked at Maggie while both women squealed, "She's pregnant!"

"Oh my gosh, Abigail, you're going to be a mother! This is wonderful. Have you told Aunt Margaret?" Lydia asked.

"I haven't even told my husband." Moaning softly from her resting place, Abigail struggled to sit up. "Darling, we're going to have a baby."

Cole sank to the mattress, his mouth hanging open in shock. "Are you sure about this, Abby?"

"I am as sure as a woman can be about something like this." Flinging her arms around his neck, she hugged her husband close. "We're going to be a family."

Tears welled up in her eyes as Maggie's heart sang for joy. Knowing how important family was to both Abigail and Cole, she was deliriously happy for them.

"Maybe we should leave them alone." Taking hold of Lydia's elbow, Alexander led them from the jail.

Waving over her shoulder, Maggie warned good-naturedly, "You'd best go up to the house. You know how news travels in this town. Aunt

Margaret is going to want to hear this from you."

"I know. Come on, Papa, let's go share our news." With the help of her husband, Abigail got up.

A pang struck Maggie as she watched the blissfully happy couple walk down Main Street. She didn't begrudge them their happiness. Seeing them made her realize that what she wanted could be right there in front of her.

"Are you all right?" Samuel fell into step beside her.

Forcing a smile, she answered, "I'm perfectly fine. And overjoyed for Abigail and Cole."

"Then why do you look like you're going to cry?"

Maggie turned to him. "I didn't get a chance to answer your question earlier. Yes, we do have a future together because I'm falling in love with you, Samuel Clay."

He was dumbfounded. She was in love with him? "Maggie, are you sure about this?"

"Oh, Samuel, of course I'm sure."

"Then you should know I feel the same way about you." Pulling her into his arms, he breathed in the fresh scent of her. "I love you, Maggie," he whispered in her ear.

Throwing her arms around his neck, she held him tightly. "How did this happen?"

"I don't know. I've been asking myself that question for a few days."

"I think this calls for a celebration!"

Letting go of him, Maggie hurried down the street ahead of him.

Calling after her, he shouted, "Hey, where are you off to?"

"You'll see."

For a very long time she'd been content with last year's castoffs. Being in love made her feel like a different person and now she wanted to look different on the outside too. She could count on one hand the number of dresses she'd purchased over the past two years. She knew it was deplorable, but she'd never considered fashion her strong suit.

Having been more focused on being a self-made independent woman, fashion trends were the last thing on her life's list of things to accomplish. Being sharp about running a business, even if it was just a small town dance hall, had become a priority.

As loathe as she was to admit it, the day Samuel Clay came into her life all of those beliefs had begun to change. Oh, she still wanted to be a successful businesswoman. The only difference now was that she didn't want to do it alone.

By the time Maggie arrived at the house, the family had gathered around Abigail and Cole. Maggie had never seen Aunt Margaret looking as happy as she did right now. It was as if the news of the baby had breathed new life into her.

"Maggie!" she called to her from the front parlor where they had assembled. "Isn't this wonderful news? Just think, by next year this time we'll have another member of the Monroe family."

Trying to hide her blissful state from her family was going to be hard, but she wanted to tell them in her own way about her and Samuel.

Lydia was looking at her in a funny way. Crossing the room she came to join Maggie by their aunt's side. "Is everything all right?"

Nodding, Maggie worked at putting a frown on her face. "I'm fine. It's just all this excitement must be getting to me."

"I don't think it's the excitement at all, Maggie. I think Samuel Clay is getting under your skin."

Her head snapped up and she met her cousin's penetrating stare. "This isn't about him," she lied, a little white lie. "Lydia, it's about me."

Lydia's mouth formed an "oh" and Maggie

saw the realization hit her. "I see. Well, is there anything I can do to help?"

"No, I can deal with this problem on my own." Gazing at the sheriff and her husband, Maggie had to smile. They were so happy.

Turning back to Lydia, she said, "I'm going to my room for a little while."

"Are you sick?" Her voice laced with concern, Lydia rested her hand on Maggie's arm.

Hugging her, Maggie replied, "I'm not sick, just a little weary." When Lydia pulled back and frowned at her, Maggie added, "Really, there's nothing to worry about."

Gathering her skirts, she headed up the stairs to her room. Upon entering, the first thing she did was open up every dresser drawer. Throwing open the doors to the wardrobe, she began an inventory.

This was the beginning of the end. Out with the old and in with the new. Oh, she could spend the rest of the day coming up with simple little sayings, but the fact of the matter was, it was about time she had a make over.

Starting with her dresser, she emptied out every last drawer on top of the bed. Then sorting through all the scarves, stockings, and undergarments, she tossed anything that was more than a year old into a heap on the floor.

Once that was finished, she started on the wardrobe. Black dresses and brown ones too soon joined the pile. When the wardrobe was finally empty she turned, placing her hands on her hips to survey the mess. And what a mess it was. Thank goodness her family was distracted by Abigail's news, thought Maggie.

What her cousins would make of this Maggie could only imagine. Truth be told, though, she was glad she didn't have to explain her actions to them because at the moment she wasn't sure herself what she was doing. A light knocking on the bedroom door brought her out of her reverie.

She opened the door just far enough to see who was on the other side. If it were either one of her cousins she would most certainly not be admitted. Surprisingly, it wasn't Abigail or Lydia standing out in the hallway.

"Mrs. Clay. How are you?" Bracing the door against the toe of her shoe, Maggie stood fast.

"Maggie, I'm sorry to be a bother, but might I have a word with you?"

Maggie started to sneak out the door, but when she was about to step out into the hallway, Mrs. Clay stopped her.

"Please, might we speak in your room?"

Glancing over her shoulder at the mess, Maggie winced. "You'll have to excuse the mess." Pulling the door open, she stepped aside, allowing Samuel's mother to enter.

The woman emitted a small gasp before quickly recovering. "I see I've caught you in the middle of something. If this isn't a good time I can come back."

"This is as good a time as any. Here, let me clear some of these things off the bed so you can sit down." Scooping up a pile of lacy petticoats and stockings, she tossed them unceremoniously on the floor.

Frowning at her, Mrs. Clay sat gingerly on the edge of the mattress. "Are you sure I'm not intruding?"

Pushing the remaining undergarments aside, Maggie made some more room, sitting next to her. "You are not bothering me. I was just going through my wardrobe. You know, a sort of late spring cleaning."

Looking at the clothing strewn about, the woman smiled. "I've been doing a little of that myself. It's one of the reasons I came to see you. I find that I'm in need of some fashion advice."

It was all she could do not to burst out laughing. This was so ludicrous, Mrs. Clay coming to her for fashion advice when she didn't have any idea on where to begin herself.

Sucking in a deep breath, she exhaled, saying,

"Mrs. Clay, I don't think there's much I can give you in the way of advice." Sweeping her arm in front of them, she added, "As you can see, I appear to be in as much of a quandary about clothing styles as you are. I'm sorry."

"Don't be sorry, Maggie." A pixyish smile played around the corners of her mouth. "Would you like to accompany me to Albany? I'm going shopping."

Hesitating, Maggie wondered at the woman's courage. Here she was, fresh off the farm and wanting to improve herself, while Maggie, who grew up in the arms of relative comfort, didn't have a clue where to begin with her own changes.

"I've already checked the train schedule and asked about accommodations. If you can be ready in an hour's time, we could leave this afternoon."

What was she waiting for? Her clothing was tossed about, much like her life felt at this moment. A few days away could be just what she needed. Laying her hand over Mrs. Clay's, she said, "I can be ready."

Samuel's mother embraced her. "We're going to have so much fun!"

Maggie didn't know about having fun. Like every other challenge she tackled in her life, her mind was already busy making lists.

The first item was telling Samuel that she would be going to Albany with his mother. Deciding she wasn't up to facing him or all the questions, Maggie went to the desk and hastily scribbled a note to him. She would ask his brother to deliver it.

Chapter Seventeen

Walter delivered the note to his brother as he was instructed to do—after the train left Surprise. Right now Walter was facing his older brother who looked angrier than a disrupted hornets' nest.

"What is the meaning of this?" Samuel sputtered.

Shuffling his feet nervously from side to side, Walter replied, "They've gone off together."

"For three days?" Sam shouted.

"It's not that long, Samuel. They're going to Albany."

"I know where they've gone!" Crumpling up the stationery, he tossed it on the floor. "My mother and Maggie alone for three days," he mumbled, pacing in front of his brother. Good God, what kind of trouble would they get in to? More importantly, he thought, what secrets of his would they share? Oh, he didn't like this one bit, not one bit. It was never good when women got together, especially when one was his mother and the other—well, the other was Maggie.

"Why did they need to go shopping in Albany? Can't they get what they need right here at the mercantile?" he wanted to know.

Since Walter didn't know a thing about women, he didn't reply, just shrugged his shoulders.

"This is just dandy!" Stomping out the door, he was tempted to march right up to the big house and find out what Miss Margaret knew. She probably put the two women up to their little sojourn.

"Walter, did they say anything other than what was in the note?" Samuel turned around to find Walter right at his heels.

"Nope. Just handed it to me and told me when to give it to you."

Samuel resumed pacing on the walkway in front of the dance hall. Every few minutes he'd stop to glance up at Miss Margaret's house, wondering if he should go up there.

Out of the corner of his eye, he caught a

glimpse of their father coming down the pebbled path leading from Miss Margaret's place.

"Good day, boys."

"Hello, Father," he muttered.

"Been standing around here long?"

"Not too long, Pa. I gave Sam the note from Miss Maggie and Ma."

His father's brows shot up. "I see. Nice the way Miss Maggie's befriended your mother isn't it, Samuel?"

Scowling at his father, he almost didn't reply and then said, "No. I don't think it's nice." Raking his hand through his hair in frustration, he stepped away from them.

Behind him he heard his father tell his brother he'd like a word with him. As Walter walked off in the direction of the mercantile, Sam felt his father's touch on his arm.

"If you're so worried about the womenfolk, why don't you go after them?"

Spinning around, he looked into his father's eyes as sheer panic gripped him. Going after those two would be far worse than staying put.

Laughing in a knowing way, his father said, "I didn't think the notion of doing that would sit too well. There's nothing worse a man could do than come between two women on a mission. And from what I saw this morning, those two were on one. Been a long time since your ma has been able to purchase new things. Since we made a nice profit on our land, I guess she's entitled to spend some of the money."

"You saw them?" Sam wanted to know about every word spoken and every glance exchanged.

"Samuel, you've got to trust them. Those two weren't going off to tell each other about you, they were going shopping."

Stubbornly he refused to believe it was a simple shopping trip, but he knew if he were going to keep his sanity over the next three days, he'd best let those thoughts go.

Looking at his father, he asked, "Can I buy you a root beer? We just got some new kegs delivered."

"I'd like that, son."

They settled at a table near the windows where they could see people passing by. A silence fell between them and Samuel toyed with his glass, wondering who would be the first to break the silence.

"How long you been here, son?" his father asked, sipping at the drink while he watched the world go by on the other side of the window.

"Going on four months."

"When are you planning on leaving?"

The question caught him off guard. Staring at his father, he realized that leaving Surprise had never occurred to him. The fact of the matter was that he liked the town and was growing fond of the people in it.

Therefore his reply was simple, "I'm not leaving."

"So you're staying on with Miss Maggie?"

Shifting uneasily in his seat, Sam tried to put his feelings for the woman in perspective. She was stubborn, outspoken, and had a darn good business sense about her. She scared the life out of him.

"Maggie and I are business partners."

"She's pretty enough."

"Very. And I love her." Pushing the half empty glass to the center of the table he continued, "I told her so today. And then instead of staying here with me, she goes running off with my mother!"

"Women can be funny sometimes." Gazing out the window, his father said, "I'd like for us to start fresh. Right now, today. We can't change our pasts, son, but maybe we can make the future better."

He thought about Maggie and the things she'd said to him right after his family had shown up here out of the blue. Everyone made their own choices in life, his had just been different from what his parents had wanted.

You can't change your past, he thought, but he sure could do something about the future. Did he really want to continue on with the rest of his life not having a connection to his family? Sighing, he knew he didn't.

For years he'd thought otherwise and now he knew the time had come to make amends.

Laying his hands on the table in front of him, he studied his father. He looked tired. The life he'd left behind had taken its toll on his father. Suddenly Sam was ashamed by his actions of so long ago. He'd left a struggling family to seek out his own fortune, never caring one way or the other how their lives ended up.

"I'm sorry for leaving you with so many burdens." It was as simple as apologies came, yet it was all he could bring himself to offer this man.

"I know you are."

In this world forgiveness didn't always come easy, but today for Daniel and Samuel Clay it did.

"You've got a nice establishment here."

Relaxing a bit, he leaned back in his chair. "That we do. Maggie is great with keeping the business organized."

"Did you ever think you'd find yourself in business with a woman?"

He shook his head. "Not one like Maggie."

"You could do worse in life." Winking at him, his father added, "I think you'd best ask her to become your wife before some other man snatches her away from you."

He darn near choked on the swallow of root beer he'd just taken. The man sure didn't beat around the bush. "I wasn't thinking that far ahead."

"Well, you should be. From what I've seen, there are a lot of eligible men walking around this town. Might be just a matter of time before another one catches her eye."

He had to hand it to his father; he was a sly one. He'd easily planted the seed in Samuel's mind. Now he had to figure out a way to convince Miss Maggie that they should spend the rest of their lives together without making himself crazy.

Chapter Eighteen

The women stepped off the train and onto the platform loaded down with parcels. Behind them the conductor followed with more packages. It looked as if they'd bought out an entire store. Thankfully, Maggie had had the foresight to wire ahead to have Mr. Wagner meet them at the station with one of Aunt Margaret's carriages.

She could hardly wait to unpack all the pretty skirts with matching blouses. She'd also bought her cousins and aunt some pretty things too. The soft quilted blanket and the perfect christening dress she'd purchased for Cole and Abigail's new baby were simply the cutest.

Looking about as they stood in the shade

under the platform roof, Maggie searched the road for any sign of Mr. Wagner. Knowing how easily distracted the man could become, she thought perhaps he'd forgotten to come get them.

"Oh, look, there's Samuel. He's coming our way."

Craning her neck around for a better view, Maggie looked in the direction Emma was pointing. Sure enough, coming down the crowded street was Samuel, seated on one of Aunt Margaret's carriages.

"I wonder if he's coming to get us. I thought your aunt's friend Mr. Wagner was going to pick us up."

"He was." The parcels were growing heavy in her arms and she was quite certain that Mrs. Clay would be relieved to be rid of hers. Shifting the weight around, Maggie watched as Samuel pulled the carriage to a stop at the curb.

Tipping his hat to them, he said, "Good afternoon, ladies. Looks like you bought out every shop in Albany." Walking to his mother, he quickly relieved her of the bulk of her packages.

Kissing him on the cheek, Emma Clay looked up at her eldest son in adoration. "We would have done just that, except Maggie kept reminding me we had to carry all of this stuff on the train."

After helping him stow the remainder of the

boxes, Maggie allowed him to help her into the carriage. Since his mother was already settled in the back seat, Maggie sat up front with him.

"I'm glad you came to get us."

Pulling away from the platform, he looked out of the corner of his eye at her. "I had to fight with John over the carriage."

"Yes, he is rather proprietary when it comes to Aunt Margaret's belongings."

Slapping the reins against the horse, he asked, "Did you ever wonder if there was something more between them than just this friendship?"

"On more than one occasion my cousins and I have discussed the matter."

"And what conclusion did you come to?"

"It was none of our business."

"I see, so you don't think they would ever get married?"

"I don't know. My aunt loved her husband deeply. I suppose she might stay single to honor his memory."

"What are your thoughts on the institution of marriage?" He was smiling rather broadly, she thought, much like the cat who'd swallowed the canary.

Her heartbeat quickened and her stomach began to flutter. If what she was hoping came true, Sam was going to propose to her!

"I hired my brother to help out with cleaning and odd jobs." Turning his head a little to the side, he looked at her. "I hope that's all right with you."

His mother spoke up from the back seat. "I think hiring Walter is a wonderful idea. It will be good for him to get to know his older brother again. He was so young when you left, Samuel."

"We needed some extra help and I'm glad your brother can help us out." Maggie was having trouble keeping up with him. One minute he was talking about marriages and the next he was discussing business.

"Father has been looking for a place for you to rent. I think Mr. Jules—he owns the mercantile," he explained to him mother, "will have some rooms to let by the end of next week."

"This is wonderful news, Samuel!"

Maggie kept glancing at him. She couldn't help it; any minute now she expected him to come back around to the subject at hand, which was their relationship!

The carriage slowed as they started the ascent up the curving drive to Aunt Margaret's house. They jostled about and Maggie bumped against Samuel's shoulder.

Smiling apologetically, he said, "Sorry. The reins slipped from my hands."

"Samuel, is everything all right? You seem a bit . . . I don't know, distracted."

"You drive me to distraction and I'm just delighted you're home."

"For goodness sake! I was gone for three days, in Albany of all places. Not too far and certainly not long enough for you to have missed me."

A feeling of unease began to work its way up her spine. Something was definitely amiss here. First he spoke of marriage and then he went on and on about the hall. This could only mean one thing—trouble, and she knew in what form. "Are those flashy dancing girls coming back here? Because if you've gone ahead and scheduled them without consulting with me first, I'll . . ." she huffed. "Well, I'll be angry at you."

Crossing her arms over her chest, she added stubbornly, "We had an agreement, Samuel."

Calmly pulling the carriage to a stop in front of the steps, he said, "Yes, we did, Maggie, and I haven't done anything to break it."

Quirking an eyebrow at him, she asked, "Are you sure?"

"Cross my heart." He ran his finger lightly over his chest, marking his heart.

"Then tell me why you look so . . ." Sweeping her hand in the air, she finished, "so happy."

Throwing his head back, he began to laugh.

"Stop that right this instant."

Settling down a bit he finally said to her, "Is there something wrong with being happy, Maggie? I mean it, have you ever been so happy with your lot in life that you thought you just might burst from the feeling of it?"

Glancing over her shoulder she saw Emma leaning forward in the seat. She was watching the two of them with keen interest.

"Must we have this conversation in front of your mother?" Two could play at this little game.

He looked surprised to be reminded that she was still in the carriage. Jumping down from the seat, he offered, "Here, Mother, let me help you down and then I can bring in these packages for you."

Accepting his hand, she smiled up at him. "Thank you dear, such a gentleman you are."

Maggie stayed in the carriage, watching him squire his mother and all those bundles into the house. They'd had a great deal of fun together. She found out that it had been years since Emma had been in Albany and even longer since she'd had the means with which to buy new things for herself.

Of course it soon became apparent that Emma Clay had a penchant for buying. She was generous to a fault with her husband and younger son, even managing to find an outrageously colorful vest for Samuel.

Maggie had fully intended to limit her own purchases to three new outfits. However, Emma's enthusiasm was contagious and she soon found herself with five brand new, ready-made dresses, complete with all the accessories right down to matching shoes.

Both women were proud of the fact that there wasn't a brown or black piece of fabric to be found in either of their wardrobes. They were so alike and yet they had their differences too.

Maggie was far more stubborn and set in her ways than Emma Clay was. Emma could forgive a person anything, even going so far as to absolve her eldest son of wrongdoing for leaving them behind all those years ago.

She could learn a thing or two from the woman. Like how not to hold on to a grudge and perhaps how to be more giving and loving when it came to relationships with the opposite gender.

So lost was Maggie in her musings, she hadn't even heard Samuel approaching, and looked up to find him standing by the side of the carriage.

"Might I help you down?"

Taking his hand, she allowed him to help her to the ground. When she went to pull away, he took hold of both of her hands, pulling her in close to him. She bumped against his broad chest.

"Samuel?" He was going to ask her right here, right now, to marry him, she just knew it!

"Maggie, I've missed you."

"I've missed you too." There was a look in his eyes she'd never seen before, a warmth which seemed to spread from his eyes across his face, making her feel all tingly inside.

Taking her hand, he started to lead her away from the front steps. They were heading in the direction of the bridal path which wound around the house, trailing off into the woods.

Her knees quivered in anticipation. How romantic was his proposal going to be, here along the beautiful pathway so aptly named.

Squeezing her hand in his, he grinned. It was becoming clear to her that he'd undergone some sort of transformation over the past three days. It was almost as if he'd finally come to terms with his past and all that brought him here to Surprise in the first place.

"I have some news. Alexander has some land that he's willing to sell me at a reasonable price to build on."

Pulling him up short, Maggie's heart pounded in her chest. "You're going to build a house?"

He shrugged. "Sometimes things like this

strike like lightening. I was talking with my father and he helped me see that all the things I want and need in my life are right here."

"I'm so glad you want to stay here."

"I have a business here, Maggie, and then there *is* you."

They'd stopped walking amidst a patch of daisies. The tall thin stalks of white blooms swayed in the afternoon breeze. Looking past his shoulder way off in the distant horizon she could glimpse the end of the Catskill Mountain range.

Slowly she worked her gaze back to him, waiting for the question. "Is there anything else you wish to tell me?"

"I love you." He brought his face in close to hers, his penetrating stare reaching into her soul and capturing her heart.

Sighing against him, she swayed slightly. "I love you, Samuel. You've waited a very long time to find a home."

"I want the house to be built before I take a wife."

Those certainly were not the words she'd been longing to hear. "I see." Stepping away from him, she felt the moment sliding away.

"I've been thinking about a lot of things while you were away. For one thing, I never imagined myself having a woman for a business partner."

"I think it worked out well for both of us. We found each other."

"Yes, we sure did."

"Samuel, isn't there something you'd like to ask me?" she prompted.

"You aren't very patient, are you?"

Shaking her head, she waited with bated breath.

He shifted his weight from one foot to the other, looking uneasy and nervous, like a man who was having second thoughts or getting a severe case of cold feet.

The bottom fell out of her stomach. He wasn't going to pop the question after all.

Embarrassment for even daring to think he might propose marriage made her pull away from him. Casting her eyes to the ground, she impulsively gathered up her skirts and ran back down the path toward the house.

He called out to her. Ignoring the sound of his voice, she let herself in the back door and raced up the servants' stairway into her bedroom.

Anna had seen to emptying the carriage of her belongings. All of the wrapped and tied boxes were placed neatly on her bed. Thinking it would be oh so satisfying to throw them all on the floor, Maggie had to clasp her hands together to keep from doing just that.

Wiping the tears from her face, she carefully removed every item from its box and put it away. Somehow the joy of the trip had gone away and in its place was deep, deep heartache the likes of which she'd never felt before.

Chapter Nineteen

"What have you done to my cousin?"

Turning toward his accuser, Sam faced Lydia head on. "I'm not sure."

He was in the front parlor of their home, sipping at a glass of tasteless lemonade. It figured that he fixed things with his family only to ruin them with Maggie. Life was strange that way.

"Did you ask her to marry you?"

"I thought that's what I was about to do."

"What did you say to her and tell me everything, word for word. If I'm going to figure out where you went wrong I'll need to know every last bit." Flopping down on the overstuffed sofa, Lydia settled down for a long chat.

"We were walking down the bridal path. I was telling her how I was going to buy the land from your husband."

Picking at a leftover butter cookie, she nodded. "Go on."

"She seemed to like the idea enough."

"Did you tell her the land would be for both of you to build your house on?" Green eyes flashed at him.

"I said I was going to build a house there."

Shaking her head, she reached for another cookie. "Well, there's your first mistake."

"Look, Lydia, I've never done anything like this before."

"I should hope not!"

"I love Maggie and I want to spend the rest of my life with her."

"Why didn't you tell her that?"

"I told her I liked having a woman as my business partner. And I was about to tell her how much she means to me and how I love her, except she ran away and now she won't come out of her room."

"You told her she was a good business partner. Excuse me for saying so, Samuel, but that wasn't very romantic of you." Rolling her green eyes heavenward, Lydia jumped up so fast Sam almost dropped the glass he'd been holding on to.

"I'll go have a few words with her."

Running after her, Sam caught her just before she was about to go upstairs. "Don't do this, Lydia. Maggie and I need to work this out on our own." He didn't know why, but it was important they see it through without interference from their well-meaning families.

"All right. But you must promise you'll come to me if you need any more advice."

"Promise." He accepted her peck on the cheek and walked her to the door. "And Lydia?"

"Yes?"

"Thank you."

"You're welcome." Before she was completely out the door, he could have sworn he heard her saying, "Don't keep us waiting too long."

He paced around the hallway for a bit, angry at himself for being such a coward when it came to love. Frankly, he'd been scared. Marrying Maggie would mean the end of his wanderlust. On the other hand, the thought of living without her was even worse to consider.

He was such a fool in love.

Propping an elbow on the newel post at the bottom of the staircase, he pondered his predicament. There was always the ogre's way of handling the situation, which would be to go upstairs and pound on Maggie's door until she opened it.

Or he could go out to Miss Margaret's rose garden and pick a bunch of roses, then present them to Maggie on bended knee.

The grandfather clock in the great room chimed the half hour and Samuel still hadn't reached a decision.

Upstairs in her bedroom Maggie began unpacking the new clothes. After she'd put away the pretty silky chemises and the soft hosiery, all that remained on the bed was the gorgeous sapphire blue evening gown. It was the priciest garment she'd ever purchased. Fingering the satin material, she was glad she'd splurged.

Taking off her traveling clothes, she stepped into the gown. The dress fit her like a glove. Running her hands down the front, then plucking at the three-quarter length sleeves, Maggie thought the only thing missing was a hair adornment. Rushing over to the dressing table, she opened a rosewood jewelry box. Nestled in the lining was a pearl-encrusted hair comb.

Quickly pulling the pins from her hair, she brushed the long locks out. Then gathering her hair off to one side, she placed the comb. Swishing to the left and then to the right, Maggie thought she looked stunning. The finishing touch would be the matching pearl necklace her father had given her on her sixteenth birthday.

With one final glance back at the mirror, she walked out of her bedroom.

Pausing at the top of the staircase, she saw Samuel sitting on the bottom step. His elbows resting on his knees, she could tell he was lost in thought. Her skirt swished as she started down. Hearing her, he turned.

She would carry the look on his face in her heart forever. His mouth opened slightly and in his eyes, oh those handsome green eyes, was the look of desire. But more than that she saw a radiant look of adoration and love.

Standing, he rested one foot on the next riser and waited for her to reach him. Deliberately, Maggie took her sweet time, letting him take in every nuance of her.

When she finally stood face to face with him, she paused.

"Samuel, I don't know what happened with us while we were on the bridal path, but I'm going to say this only one time. I love you, and if you'll have me for your wife, I'd like for us to be married."

His look became quite serious then and for one frightening moment she thought he might turn down her offer. Straightening her spine, Maggie held her ground. Looking at him, she knew there was no other man on this earth for her.

"I'm not going to take no for an answer." She'd meant to make a bold statement, but instead the words came out in a whisper.

Taking hold of her hands, he said, "Then I guess I'll have to agree to become your husband. But before I do I want to tell you that you are my life. Every breath I take from this day forward will be for you."

"Such fancy words coming from you," she said, feeling the first tear falling from her eyes.

His pale eyebrows rose. "Oh, and did I tell you how beautiful you look?"

Shaking her head, she replied, "You must have forgotten."

"Maggie Monroe, you are the most beautiful woman I know. Maggie, I'm sorry about earlier. I don't know what happened to me."

Laughing and crying at the same time, she fell into his arms. "Lucky for you, Mr. Clay, I forgive easily."

Of course they both knew how stubborn she could be. Excitement coursed through her, causing her to begin babbling, "You know, come to think of it, you're really not my type. I don't even know why I fell in love with you. I do know that once I did there was no turning back."

"Maggie, stop talking," he whispered.

Gently pulling her down the stairs, he gathered her up and began to hum the same waltz tune he'd used when he taught her to dance. Before she knew what was happening, they were waltzing around her aunt's foyer.

"How did I get to be so lucky?"

"You came to Surprise. Didn't you know good things happen to people here, Samuel?"

"Indeed they do." Bending his head, he placed his lips upon hers, drinking in their warmth.

They swayed together to music only they could hear. Leaning his head back, he looked at her once more. "We're going to make beautiful children together."

"Who said anything about children?" she asked, wearing a smirk.

"I did. We should have at least four of them. There's a good even number."

"Ah, my Samuel, always putting the cart before the horse."

Chapter Twenty

From the edge of the bridal path Margaret Monroe Sinclair stood, aided by neither a wheelchair nor a cane, thinking about how her life had come full circle. On the wings of a promise she'd settled in this small, unassuming town of Surprise as a young bride full of hope.

Seasons had come and gone. Her husband had left her with a legacy of hope for the future. And Margaret hadn't disappointed his memory, for single-handedly, or so she liked to think, she'd brought this town back from the brink of obscurity.

The town of Surprise, surrounded by the beauty of the Catskill Mountains, was filling with new business ventures and young families. Her own family had doubled in size. Turning at the sound of laughter, she smiled at the sight of Abigail with her rounding belly, hugging her husband Cole close.

Lydia and Alexander were standing by the long refreshment tables set up under the apple tree, helping their children pile their plates with food.

And lastly there was Maggie, the toughest of the lot. She and her new husband stood side by side greeting their wedding guests.

"Miss Margaret, are you happy?"

Her lifelong friend John Wagner had slipped next to her unnoticed. "I'm very happy, John."

Wiggling his thick, springy eyebrows at her, he said, "You certainly accomplished all that you set out to do. I wouldn't have thought it possible."

Folding her arms in front of her, she frowned at him. "With enough courage and foresight, anything is possible, John."

"Margaret, you have enough of those sentiments for the entire town."

Pride welled up inside of her bringing a rush of unexpected tears to her eyes. "I love this place and now I know the town of Surprise will be here for generations to come."

The sun began its descent behind the Catskill Mountains. In the pink haze of evening tide, birds chirped merrily while butterflies danced from one flower to the next seeking the sweet nectar. And as twilight began to settle in, a small town celebrated the continuation of life.